"D'Amato retains her touch for red herrings in a tantalizing puzzle."

—*Chicago Sun-Times*

"D'Amato draws a compelling picture of street life in a very recognizable Chicago."

—*Chicago Tribune*

"Gripping and poignant, *Hard Women* provides a fresh view of the world's oldest profession."

—*Baltimore Sun*

"...the denouement in an El station late at night is a real heart-stopper."

—*Los Angeles Times*

"...a harrowing and compelling portrait of life on Chicago's mean streets. A wonderful mystery with a sudden and exciting climax."

—Jackson, Mississippi *Clarion-Ledger*

"The series about Cat Marsala is one of the best to debut in recent years...."

—*The Armchair Detective*

"Highly recommended."

—*Mystery News*

"Mystery fans who enjoy seeing a moral dilemma through to its satisfactory conclusion are bound to relish this one."

—*Mostly Murder*

Barbara D'Amato

Hard Women

W⊕RLDWIDE®

TORONTO • NEW YORK • LONDON
AMSTERDAM • PARIS • SYDNEY • HAMBURG
STOCKHOLM • ATHENS • TOKYO • MILAN
MADRID • WARSAW • BUDAPEST • AUCKLAND

HARD WOMEN

A Worldwide Mystery/August 1994

This edition is reprinted by arrangement with Charles
Scribner's Sons, an imprint of Macmillan Publishing
Company.

ISBN 0-373-26150-0

To Commander Hugh Holton,
Chicago Police Department, whose vast
knowledge of police work is equaled only by his
generosity in sharing his expertise

ONE

DOES ANYBODY CARE about a dead hooker?

I was on my way home on the El after a hard day. When you work freelance as a reporter, any day without a good haul of usable interviews and quotable quotes and pithy data is a hard day. A day *with* them is even harder. I'd put in a lot of time at the library, then half an hour at the Chicago Police Department with my buddy Harold McCoo, then spent hours talking with a variety of streetwalkers.

It was ten P.M. The El, which runs past my apartment building, screamed to a halt and paused long enough to let five of us off. There were two women wearing housedresses and carpet slippers through which their bunions peeked, who were probably cleaning women just finished with some Loop offices. There was a third woman, in expensive shoes (no visible bunions) and a drop-dead fur, who went tap-tapping quickly away from the station. There was a man in a light wool suit carrying a slender briefcase and wearing a satisfied expression. And there was me, wearing a Cubs jacket and carrying a notepad and twenty or thirty pens and pencils in my pocket.

I had hardly started down from the top of the El steps when the train accelerated with the sound of a Boeing-747 crash-landing on concrete. Every moving part of an El train is steel, and as far as you can tell from the noise, none of it is lubricated. I hear it all night from my apartment. Somehow, it spells home.

At the bottom of the steps, half a block from my apartment, I caught a glimpse of the flashing whip-whip-whip of Mars lights on squad cars up ahead. This is not uncommon around here, and I wasn't worried. If anything, I was thinking about what to do with my house-guest. I had inherited a prostitute who was staying with me because she had nowhere else to go. Her name was Sandra Lupica, but she liked to be called Sandra Love. The current dilemma was how to get rid of her nicely. Charity begins at home. But my question in this case was Where does it end?

As I drew nearer my place, I saw that the squads, three of them, were at the alley just past my building. One was nosed in, the other two were drawn up parallel to the curb in the street, and two uniforms stood in the street motioning cars past and generally preventing gaper's block.

This was too close. It began to worry me.

The crowd was still very small, maybe twenty people. Chicago-style curiosity usually draws an audience pretty fast. Sliding along the brick wall of the building that cornered on the street and alley, I edged around the crowd and came up to the crime scene.

A woman wearing a green spangly blouse lay sprawled on her back on the pavement. Her head was on the lip of the curb and her chestnut hair flowed over the curb and into the water that pooled sluggishly in the shallow alley gutter. Her glittery silver bag lay next to her; her skirt was too short; her makeup was just a bit too much. Everything about her said "hooker." Oh, Lord! It was Sandra.

During the afternoon and evening I had thought a dozen times about how to get her to leave and go back to her own place. I had been thinking about the problem ten minutes earlier on the train. Maybe I had been thinking that at the very moment she was dying.

A lab man approached the body with his camera and started briskly snapping photos from several sides. A detective in plain clothes said a word or two to one of the uniforms, shrugged, and turned away. I know they see death all the time. I know they can't become emotionally involved. But it looked to me as if the unspoken message was "This woman isn't a valuable member of society."

Or was it just my feeling of guilt?

TWO

FOUR DAYS EARLIER, Tuesday, September 8, I was at Branch 40, or Women's Court, familiarly known as hooker court, at Eleventh and State. Hooker court is supposed to get underway at ten A.M. But an observer would be lucky to see any cases called before eleven. I had arrived at nine-thirty, knowing I was early, because I wanted a seat in front.

I had come intentionally on Tuesday, the morning after the Labor Day weekend. Women arrested after Friday noon and not bonded out would have sat around in the cells until today, since the judges went home at noon on Fridays before vacations. This meant that some of the women who would come to court this morning had been in jail here in the building for four days. The women's jail is on the thirteenth floor of the building, hooker court on eight. There is a men's jail on eleven, two other courts in the building, plus the First District Police Station, but most of the building houses the central offices of the Chicago Police Department, the Big Cop Shop.

However, I'd come for the women. It's going to sound heartless when I say that I wanted a hungry hooker, but that's the way it was. I wanted to take one of the women to lunch, and I wanted her grateful enough to talk.

The thirteenth floor of this building is the top floor. When a prostitute is arrested in the area covered by the First District, which is roughly the South Loop, the officers say they're taking her to the penthouse, because the jail is on the top floor. That is all that is penthouse-like about the place, though.

The building was built in the twenties and nothing much has happened to the cells since that time. There are three long banks of cells, usually one woman per cell. It would seem to be private accommodations, but you can hear everything through the bars that cover the front of the cell. The noise is constant—crying, cursing, retching, metal doors slamming. The "cot" on which you sleep is made of four two-by-six boards, varnished once upon a time, now polished by generations of bodies. The guards take the woman's shoes away and put them outside the cell. They take her belt away. They don't give her a blanket, probably for fear she may hang herself, but the jail is kept very warm. The woman sleeps in her clothes, if she can sleep.

Meals are served three times a day. Lunch is a bologna sandwich on white bread. Dinner is a bologna sandwich on white bread. Breakfast is a bologna sandwich on white bread. If the guards are feeling especially kindly, they will heat the bologna sandwiches in their microwave. Warm bologna sandwiches on white bread.

Absolutely nothing else happens. There is no television, no coffee break, no entertainment except the shrieks and curses of other women.

After four days of this, my potential targets would probably want two things more than anything else—a hot bath and a good dinner. I wasn't going to provide the hot bath, but if somebody would accept my offer, I would buy her dinner. Steak, Italian, Chinese, whatever she wanted.

All she had to do was talk to me.

A fly buzzed against the window near me. He was joined by a wasp. The wasp struck the glass, then bumped his way down the pane, finally ending in the lower corner, sputtering hopelessly, unable to get out.

Was this a metaphor for the people who would soon be coming into court?

There didn't seem to be anybody around to care—just a couple of black pimps who were too young or inexperienced to realize that the women they were here to bond out wouldn't be brought to court this early. So I got up and tried to raise the window. It was stuck in place, petrified by layers and layers of institutional paint—cream, gray, pale green, khaki, and apparently once sky blue. Plus way down deep in the worst scratches, traces of wood, stained dark.

Both the fly and the wasp had flown away while I tried to lift the window.

I went back to my seat. The pimps looked at me idly. They were young, but they'd seen plenty of nutty people in the world already. As a matter of fact, they'd probably seen plenty of strange people already today. I was just another one.

By now some of the cast was assembling. A Tweedledum and Tweedledee pair of bailiffs walked from the back to the front with the rolling gait of persons with fat thighs.

Lawyers appeared, a couple of them expensive in three-piece suits that cost more than my car, some cheap in bright suits highlighted by gold bracelets and gold watches and, in one case, a sparkling stickpin. Stickpin? Didn't stickpins go out with spats? They must have come back. There was one tall, cadaverous white man with white hair who wore a dark green velvet suit and a frilled shirt. I spent an idle couple of minutes trying to guess whether he was a lawyer, a friend of one of the women arrested, a pimp, or the owner of an escort service.

Maybe I'd find out when his "client's" case came up.

The room had windows all along two sides, east and south. Already, with the sun high in the sky, it was starting to warm up. A bailiff went around pulling down the shades. They were yellowed fabric, very much like the ones in my old grade school and apparently of the same vintage, water stained, brown and frayed on the edges. The bailiff pulled them down by cords that he wound around cleats on the sill.

We were high tech here in this court.

Now the glow from the morning sun was filtered through the shades, casting the room into a sulfurous gloom, making us all look like victims of liver disease.

Two youngish women and a very young man drifted in and made their way to a table at the front, near the judge's bench, but over against the wall. From the place where they set up shop, I knew these were the public defenders, here to shepherd the cases where the defendant had no lawyer. The public defenders tended to be young because in this court they quickly became burned out.

The room by now was humming with conversations. The front-row seats were all full, and the back filling fast. Bunches of people were standing around in the rear, wheeling and dealing. This court had a reputation for shady characters: There are lawyers who hang around the corridors outside, catching relatives of the defendants as they come in, offering to take cases for a fee. Their sales pitch was "You don't want a public defender, do you?" Some may actually do better for a client than the overworked public defenders—maybe—but most don't. They all demand cash up front.

Every once in a while some man in a suit will take fees from the relatives or pimps of several defendants about to come before the judge and then skip. Vanish. Not be there at all when the case is called. Such a man is a scammer. A shark, living off the weak and wounded.

Finally, the judge entered. Black robe, gray hair, the whole schmear. His eyelids hung down at the outside corners. He looked very, very tired.

Court was in session, the honorable Ewan Mestrovic presiding.

Here we go, I thought. They call it the cattle call.

The first woman out was accompanied by a guard, but the guard really didn't need to guard anything. The woman was white, with stringy orange hair, about forty-five by my best guess, though she looked sixty. Drooping mouth, drooping hair, drooping jowls, and a short-short skirt drooping on one side and showing a lot of thigh on the other. She couldn't have fought her way out of a puff of cigarette smoke, much less the courtroom. Every once in a while she would give a sudden twitch, as if a small bug had bitten her. Otherwise, she didn't look at anybody.

As she and the guard emerged from the prisoners' door, a strange odor entered the courtroom. It was more than Lysol and sweat and dirt; it was a blend of those and something that smelled like age, and a sour tang of fear. It was the odor of the lockup. Because I was in the front row, I smelled it clearly.

The woman was too defeated to be a good interviewee, I thought, as the charge of solicitation was read. In a way, I would like to talk with her. I'd like to know what she was thinking. It always surprised me the number of women who were much too old for the prostitution game but went on no matter what. I realize they may not know any other trade, but it would seem the insults would grow to be too much and the falling prices make it useless to keep on trying.

But that wasn't exactly my assignment right now. Plus, it was early in the morning and there'd be lots to choose from. And tomorrow and the next day.

The parade would go on and on, day after day.

The woman had no pimp or lawyer waiting for her. An independent operator, no doubt. She was way under the economic floor where anybody would bother trying to live off her earnings. A public defender spoke to her briefly, muttering her rights in her ear. She shrugged. Finally, she responded, "Guilty."

The judge said, "Two hundred dollars fine or three days in jail, and you have had blood drawn for an AIDS test?"

"Yes, your honor."

"I see you were arrested Sunday. Two day's allowance. Fine or one day in jail."

She took the jail, probably because she didn't have two hundred dollars.

The next woman out was quite a different proposition. Tall, black, slender, *big* hair. She wore silver boots. Her gold-shot Lycra spandex top showed no wrinkles, but then spandex doesn't show wrinkles. The hot pants did. But from the way she carried it off, you'd think wrinkles were high fashion. An equally flashy white lawyer leaped to his feet as he heard her name called.

He bounded to the bench. The arresting officer walked up more slowly, and stood on the right. The state's attorney stood on the left. The woman acknowledged she had had blood drawn.

I was all ready to hear a spirited defense.

"Loitering for purposes of solicitation." The prosecutor commented that she had four other arrests on her record for the same offense. The police officer who had arrested her stood taller when his name was called. His face telegraphed "ready to testify."

She said, "Guilty."

Her lawyer paid the fine, three hundred dollars in this case, and they headed together down the courtroom aisle toward the exit. The entire exchange hadn't taken two and a half minutes. I bounded after them, terrier on the scent.

"Excuse me!"

"What do you want?" the lawyer said.

"Could I have a word with your client?"

"We'll see," he said. "Go ahead. What's your story?" He wore three pinkie rings. All on one finger.

"I'm a reporter." Instantly, they turned and walked away.

"Wait, wait! My name is Cat Marsala. I'm not trying to report your name. I'm not doing that kind of story."

"Oh, no?" the woman said.

Up close she was just as beautiful as at a distance. She wore no makeup right now. Probably washed off in the lockup. She didn't need it. Dark eyes, the whites of the eyes not bloodshot with liquor or yellow from drugs. Not yet, anyhow. When she chose to talk, the lawyer shut up and let her, which told me something. I said, "I'm doing an article for a television channel. A TV essay, they call it. On how prostitutes get along in this city. What life is like for them."

"And just why should I care?"

"I thought you might want to tell your side of things." I had angled myself around so that I stood between her and the exit corridor.

"And have my mama see me saying all this shit on Channel whatever?"

"We can give you a mask or silhouette you so people don't know it's you."

"Then I don't get famous."

"We can do it either way."

She shook her head as if people as stupid as me really shouldn't have survived this long. She glanced down the hall behind me, glanced back at me and said, "Move!"

I moved. The lawyer bustled after her.

Okay, live and learn. If I wanted to get to the high-end hookers, the really expensive types, I would have to have an intro.

Back to court.

There was a woman already walking out. Another two-minute case. She was white, very thin. There was a sore on the side of her mouth and one eye was reddish and watery. She kept clenching and unclenching her hands as she walked past me. I hesitated, staring at her, but she didn't look back, and I almost went after her. Somehow, I couldn't do it. It seemed like even touching her with my voice would give her added pain.

In the courtroom, my seat had been taken. As had all the other seats. I leaned against the wall, along with about twenty other people, most of them young males, black, white, and Hispanic.

In front of the judge was a white, maybe Hispanic woman. Maybe Italian. I hadn't heard her name. Maybe thirty. Very overweight. She must have been five feet three and weighed one-seventy. Her clothes had been made for a person five feet one who weighed one-fifty. Yes, she said, she had had blood drawn.

"One hundred dollars," the judge said.

The woman forked over one hundred dollars of her own. Somebody took her aside and pointed to some paperwork. She sighed something, nodded at something else, and by the time the next case was called she was scuffling up the aisle to the door.

I caught up with her at the door and held it for her. Gave her my spiel. Who I was, what I was doing.

She swung around and fixed me with her eyes. Without a word, she shook her head.

"Don't you understand? I want to tell *your* side," I said, frustrated.

She said, "I ain't got a side."

She had been looking past me all but that short moment, and now she scanned the lobby again. She was jumpy, and walked around me without another word. She didn't need me, probably had already forgotten I existed. She was looking for somebody to supply her with something, maybe crack, and she'd keep looking until she found it. She wouldn't stay here long. This building was primarily occupied by the Police Department.

Well, I was doing just fine here. Can you believe that some people think reporters are overpaid? After all, the argument goes, it's such a glamorous business.

Another heavy-set woman, this one black, was before the judge. There was a mean-looking guy with her, though. And I had begun to think I'd do better with women who were alone, if I had a choice. Both pimps and lawyers were likely to tell them not to talk. Or horn in on the conversation, which would be equally bad.

"Loitering with intent to solicit—"

The guy started muttering about entrapment, lack of evidence, bias on the part of the cops. He was no lawyer, but he knew the jargon. When he finished, the judge said, "Four hundred dollars or seven days in jail, and an AIDS test."

It looked like the judge gave you more time and a higher fine if you put up any sort of fight. That was all the fight this pair could muster, though. They paid.

"Sandra Lupica."

A young woman came through the door under guard. This one, too, looked like she needed guarding about as much as the judge's Kleenex box did. She had lank reddish brown hair, although it might not have been so lank whenever she was first picked up. There are no hairdressers on the thirteenth floor. She wore a plain blue shirt and a denim skirt. She also had a small brown paper bag of possessions, like most of the women carried.

The arresting officer rose from the bench and walked forward to stand on the right. The state's attorney went up near the judge on the left. A public defender, one of the two women, mumbled something to her, but she shook her head.

"Sandra Lupica. Soliciting. How do you plead?" the judge said.

So far none of the women I'd seen—not one—had offered any substantial defense. There was no sign of any claim to have been someplace else at the time, or of actually being in another line of work entirely. It was as if court time, jail time, and fines were a cost of doing business.

She was no exception. She didn't even speak. She nodded when she was asked whether she had had blood drawn.

"Your Honor," the state's attorney said.

"I wasn't asking—"

The bailiff muttered in the judge's ear.

"Ah, I see what you want to tell me, sir," the judge said.

"Yes, there's a bond forfeiture warrant out for Miss Lupica, from July, which was why she wasn't bonded out when she was first arrested on Friday—"

"I can see that," the judge said. "Miss Lupica, why didn't you appear for your hearing?"

"I, uh, I forgot." This was the first time her voice had been heard or asked for. It sounded as if she hadn't spoken since Friday.

"You forgot?"

"Your honor!" A tall man in a three-piece suit came striding in from the outside corridor, to stand in the center of the group before the judge. "Your Honor! I represent Miss Lupica."

"You're late, Counselor."

"I'm extremely sorry, Your Honor. LaSalle Street was under construction and so was the Monroe feeder ramp."

"LaSalle Street and the Monroe feeder ramp are *always* under construction."

"Yes, Your Honor. I'm sorry."

"Well, what do you have to say, Counselor?"

"We'd like to have the charge reduced from solicitation to loitering, Your Honor."

"I'm sure you would, Counselor. Is the arresting officer present?"

Since he was standing right in front of the judge, I had to assume the question was intended more in the nature of stage directions than a real question.

"Yes, Your Honor," said the police officer.

"What is your evidence?"

"Defendant came to the Lawrencia Hotel in response to my call for an escort to accompany me to a party."

"There's some entrapment here, Your Honor," the lawyer said.

"Let's just *hear* it first, Counselor."

"Uh—we had telephoned the Beau Monde Agency. We were running a random check."

"He's saying 'we,' Your Honor."

The cop said, "Another officer, Officer Barton, and I."

"Go on."

"So when she arrived at the hotel room, she offered to perform various sex acts. Without my asking."

"Doesn't sound like entrapment to me, Counselor. Sounds like she instigated it."

"Your Honor, it's just his word against hers. How do we know *he* didn't instigate it?"

"She has a record, Counselor. What about this outstanding warrant? She's forfeited bond in that case."

"Yes, Your Honor. Well, I'll guarantee she'll appear for a hearing this time if you feel a hearing is necessary. But I would like to ask, in view of the dubiousness of the evidence, that the charge be reduced to loitering—"

"Give it up, Counselor! I can hear the case on September twenty-third."

"That works for me, Your Honor," the prosecutor said, looking at his date book.

The lawyer started to say "Yes, yes, all right—" but the arresting officer said, "I'm testifying in another case that day."

"Oh. I also have the afternoon of the twenty-fifth," the judge said.

The lawyer said, "I'll have to reschedule something else, but all right."

The state's attorney and the police officer both nodded.

"The twenty-fifth. Two o'clock." The judge fixed Sandra Lupica with a beady eye. "Be there."

"Yes, sir."

There was a five-thousand-dollar bond set. The lawyer had come prepared and plunked down the five hundred dollars that made up the ten percent posted for Sandra.

"Next case."

Never mind she had a lawyer, this woman was for me. There was something interesting about her. Without doing anything, she had got my attention. I pushed away from the wall I was leaning against and followed the lawyer and Sandra Lupica out. A young black woman in a lemon-colored dress stood up in the very back of the courtroom and followed us out, too.

"May I talk to you?" I said to Sandra.

The lawyer said, "Who are you?"

Here we go again. I explained. He said, "No."

Still Sandra didn't speak for herself. Then the woman in the lemon dress came up to us and Sandra threw her arms up and they hugged. The woman said, "Oh, baby!"

"Celine!" Sandra said.

We were milling around the doors of the extremely slow, old elevators at Eleventh and State. I had time to give my entire spiel and still no elevator stopped at the eighth floor.

Then Sandra spoke. "You gonna give me cab fare?" she said to the lawyer.

"You've got a couple bucks."

"You're supposed to give me cab fare, things like this."

"We're out money because of you. You miss another hearing, honey, you'll be out on your ear." I heard the black woman mutter "Stingy bastard" under her breath. An elevator arrived. It was jammed to the point nobody else could get on. The lawyer said, "I'm in a hurry," and he pushed in anyway, using up the last few square inches of floor space and leaving us stranded. The doors closed.

"I'll buy you lunch," I said, "*and* drive you home after."

"WHY'D YOU AGREE to come with me?" I asked Sandra at the restaurant.

"Does it matter?"

"Sure it matters. Why wouldn't it?" I was getting tired of feeling that everything in her life didn't matter. So far, she responded with that remark to my question about how she was feeling and my question about whether the jail had been unpleasant. "It matters," I said. "What you think matters."

"Okay. I was curious."

"Really?"

"No. Yes. But I was also pissed off."

"That sounds more like it."

"Everybody telling me what to do. I figured they'd for sure tell me not to go anywhere with a reporter. So I did."

"Mmm-mm. Well, thanks."

Celine had also advised against coming to the restaurant with me. Sandra suddenly remembered that and said, "Not you, Celine. But you know what I mean."

Celine said, "Yeah." She thought a few seconds and said, "Yeah," again. "Well, I guess Cat's not so bad."

We were in the Roman Garden, and it was maybe half an hour before the noon rush. Not to worry. They wouldn't urge us to leave. Not with the amount of food in front of Sandra. And Celine. Actually, I was having a pretty good go at the fettuccine Alfredo myself.

I studied my lunch companions. Somehow I had got two for the price of two. Not that either of them had said word one about actually agreeing to do an interview with me. Celine had been acting protective of Sandra. Sandra had gone at the garlic bread and red wine I ordered for her exactly like a person who had been living on bologna sandwiches and lukewarm coffee for four days. I hadn't had the heart to talk business in the first moments of her single-minded attack on the lunch.

She ate everything. Salad—every lettuce leaf, scrap of anchovy, pepperoncini, crescent of onion, black olives, everything.

Celine ate well, too, but nothing like Sandra. Celine just ate like somebody who enjoys having somebody else buy dinner for her.

Looking at the two young women, I realized that I had not seen them entirely accurately in the haste and confusion of Branch 40. I had thought, for instance, that Celine was prettier than Sandra. Now it was clear that I had been deceived by the fact that Celine was dressed in pressed, clean clothes, and was carefully made up, and her hair was clean and styled. Celine was a very pretty young woman. She had big, deep brown eyes, arching eyebrows, and long eyelashes that looked real to me. But her face was not as beautiful—going by what is conventionally called pretty in the current day and age—as Sandra's. She was slightly lacking in chin, a little too rounded in the lower cheeks. She had a somewhat pear-shaped face. Celine was cute in the best, nonditzy sense of the word.

Sandra could probably be a knockout when she got it all together. Her hair was red-brown and looked stringy now, but washed and glossed up it would have been a warm chestnut. While Celine's eyes were deep brown, Sandra's were a striking sea-green. And her oval face was classic. Delicate features. Soft, silky lashes and eyebrows. A fine-boned body. Give her a little makeup and a sea-blue dress and she'd collect every eye in the place.

Right now she looked like a waif.

I said, "You two live together?"

"Jeez, no," Celine said. Sandra kept eating. "Whatever gave you that idea?"

"Nothing special. You seem like friends."

"Nah. We *are* friends. But I live with my sister."

"She have a family?"

"Oh, yeah. Three kids, one husband. I get my room, share a bathroom, pay rent. Works out."

"What about you, Sandra?"

"I got a room in an SRO."

The next question was a little awkward. After all, for all I knew Celine was a high school friend or something. "Uh, do you both, uh, work for the escort service?"

Celine rolled her eyes at the ceiling. Sandra said, "Yeah."

"Can I ask you some questions?"

Sandra said, "Sure. You're entitled." She had ordered stuffed flank steak for her main course, and we were now waiting for that, Celine and I still slowly eating our fettuccine, but I thought she was at least well fed enough so that talking with her wouldn't be cruel.

"How old are you?"

"Twenty-four."

"Uh-huh." I wrote it down. "Now. How old are you really?"

She studied me a couple of seconds. I don't know how she made decisions, but she finally said, "Nineteen."

"Your name is Sandra—"

"Sandra Love."

"Oh?" That wasn't what I'd heard in court.

"Well, it used to be Sandra Lupica, but I gave that up."

"Why?"

"It wasn't as—it didn't sound as nice. Why are you writing this down?"

"I'm not going to print it or anything. It's just to remind me. If you agree to do an interview with me, it'll be for a camera."

"A television camera?"

"Let me explain what I'm asking you to do. Or asking you to think about doing. I'm putting together a TV essay, which means the channel will show it as a kind of educational thing about prostitution in Chicago. It'll all be taped ahead of time. In the segment, I will be talking with some women, probably six or eight different women who work different ways, different levels of the business." I was beginning to get an idea of what I wanted, but it wasn't quite what the studio seemed to want. "Some of them may let us tape them as they really look, maybe with just their first names—"

"They'd be admitting to a crime, wouldn't they?" Sandra asked.

She was sharp all right. "Not necessarily. It depends on how we'd ask the question. Suppose I asked, 'How do escort services get clients?' and say the woman answered, 'Mostly the clients look in the Yellow Pages.' She'd be telling us something from her knowledge, but she wouldn't explicitly be saying she'd taken part."

She laughed. "You're gonna have to have somebody say they took part in something, or you sure don't have much of a story."

"I think I can do that. Say somebody is planning to leave the life and start over. And she says so. That's one way. Anyhow, most of my women will either talk with a small mask or with that scrambler effect where the television camera breaks up the face so you can't tell who it is."

"And they make the voice sound liii-ike thiii-iisss," Celine said suddenly, with a good imitation of television voice distortion.

"Well, I don't want them to sound like something that came from under a rock on the planet Neptune. I was talking with the producers about that, and they say they can do just a little speeding up or slowing down and maybe buff off some aspirates a little, so you don't sound like yourself."

The flank steak had arrived, and I lost Sandra's full attention.

"The whole segment will either be five minutes or seven minutes. It doesn't sound like a lot, but that's a lot of time for TV. It'll go on during the local news, like the four o'clock or the five or the ten o'clock. Maybe one of the early ones and the ten o'clock, both."

Sandra, with that abrupt decision to confide that I'd noticed before, said, "Know why I *really* decided to come to lunch with you?"

"No."

"Because I didn't have any coke in the joint there, you know. For four days. And I thought, Shit, here I am sort of a mess already, halfway off, so why not see if just eating a lot of good stuff helps."

"Does it?"

"Yeah. It really does. I've been thinking about quitting, you know? I mean, there goes any money I make and I'm never gonna get ahead at this rate. It's stupid. So I just thought, Why not see how it goes?"

"Right. Why not?"

"Course, I thought that before a few times."

"What happened?"

"Well, I'd get depressed, you know how it is. Nervous and depressed."

"Uh-huh."

"So. Then—you know."

"How'd you get into this line of work?" It sounded lame, put this way, but I was searching for a neutral phraseology. Anyway, it went down well enough with Sandra and Celine.

"Well, see—" Sandra said, exchanging a glance with Celine. The glance was the sort that asks how you can explain something to somebody who doesn't have any idea of the troubles, problems, and difficulties of your life.

"See, supposing you didn't really have anything else you knew how to do—"

"Skills," said Celine. "Supposing you didn't have any skills."

"And you had a choice of waitress or cleaning lady."

"Baby-sit, maybe," Celine said.

"But is that the whole story?" I asked both of them together. "You're both bright; you look good. What about learning other skills?"

"Well, see, suppose you didn't finish high school."

"Why?"

"Say you sort of got thrown out at home."

"Okay. Say you did. What about school now? Could you get a GED?"

"How'm I gonna pay my rent?"

This was no time to argue. I didn't want to lose them, and besides, if you haven't walked a mile in the other person's sandals— There was a lot more to Sandra's family story, no doubt.

"See, that's what I'd like to interview you about. What are the choices? When people make decisions, it's for a reason."

Sandra said, "Well, maybe." She might have meant maybe she'd do the interview or maybe people did things for reasons.

"That guy who came into court, the lawyer? Does he work for the escort service?" They both nodded. Celine caught Sandra's attention and they rolled their eyes again.

"You don't like him?" I asked.

"He's a slimeball," Sandra said.

It turned out that Sandra thought cannoli with a scoop of chocolate-chip ice cream on the side would be a nice dessert. Celine and I, both avoiding additional calories, ordered black coffee and watched her eat. I gave the probing questions a rest, and talked about food—who made the best mint-chocolate-chip ice cream in Chicago, Baskin-Robbins or Bresler's?—hoping they'd think I was a mellow, pleasant sort who would be nice to do an interview with. After a while, the waiter came with the check. Looking at it, I reflected how good it was to have a television studio willing to underwrite some expenses. The print media are cheapskates.

I paid the check.

"Tell me something," I said.

Sandra said, "Okay."

"How about another plate of cannoli and ice cream?"

She looked at me, grinning. "No. But thanks." For just a second I could see another Sandra peek out, flirtatious and spunky.

"Okay."

Celine turned to me with a considering look on her face.

"Know what I like about you?" she said.

"No. What?"

"You didn't accuse us of pretending to talk with you just to get a free lunch."

"Oh." I couldn't help smiling. "I wondered about it, you know."

"Sure. You're not a total moron."

"I'm delighted to hear you say that."

Sandra cut in. "I really will think about it. The interview. I promise."

"Here's my card." I just recently got myself cards. Made me feel like I was a grown-up. I gave one to Sandra and one to Celine, too. "My address, phone number. Call anytime. There's a machine, if I'm not there."

They nodded.

"And now, I'll keep *my* promise. I'll drive you home."

I DROVE CELINE HOME first, to a neighborhood of tiny houses northwest of the Loop, but conveniently just a block off the bus line. It was easy to imagine Celine, getting a call from the escort service, told to go to a glitzy Loop hotel, such-and-such a room, getting all silked up, putting on her evening hot clothes, walking to the bus, and going to work. What did her sister think about it? And what did her brother-in-law think about it? Did they wonder what their children saw and understood? Or were they hard pressed for cash and in no mind to think anything as long as they got their rent money?

I wanted to know, but this was not the time to ask.

Sandra's "home" was a single-room-occupancy hotel in the seedier West Loop. I had taken Celine home first, hoping Sandra would talk on the way back, but she was starting to fade. I didn't think she wanted coke right this minute, but I wasn't an expert. It looked to me as if this was a nineteen-year-old young woman who needed sleep. She'd been four nights in a loud, bright, nasty, smelly, unpleasant place, and now she'd been fed. Probably she wanted to sleep the whole day away.

"Thanks. Really," she said, getting out of the car in front of a deteriorated barbershop flanked by a currency exchange and an underwear store.

"Keep my card. Give me a call."

"Sure. I'll think about it."

Of the two, I was more interested in Sandra. She seemed more complicated, more intriguing to me than Celine. Why? Celine was more alert. Celine, I thought, was bright but directionless, the kind of person who hadn't found anything she really liked to do yet. I felt she probably hadn't had the patience to finish school. But maybe I was doing her an injustice.

Celine was very street smart and at least surface tough.

Sandra was less polished but more interesting. She had flashes of rebelliousness, papered over by a passiveness that might be an adaptation to circumstances rather than her true nature. In a way, this made her terribly vulnerable. She was the sort of person who could get into very serious trouble.

I'd interview both, if I could. But of the two, I would prefer to interview Sandra.

I couldn't figure her out. And I liked that.

THREE

BY TWO P.M., I was in the Chicago Police Department, in the office of Deputy Chief Harold McCoo.

"See, basically there's two ways to make coffee," said McCoo. "I mean two acceptable ways. There's all kinds of ways you can do it wrong, just like anything else in the world. Lotta ways to do it wrong, not so many to do it right."

"Yes, boss," I said.

"Now quit that. It's okay for the troops, but it sounds stupid coming from you."

"Continue the lecture."

"Well, you could call it the Northern European method and the Southern European method."

"Pray go on, Professor McCoo."

"You're right. 'Boss' isn't so bad."

"Go on. This way," I added, waving my coffee mug in the air, "isn't half bad, whichever it is."

"It's really a question of roasting. The Northern European way, which is also the way most of the American coffee manufacturers do it, is what you might call the light roast. People who prefer it say that they retain more of the flavor of the coffee bean that way. And there's much to be said for that point of view."

We were in the Big Cop Shop, Central Police Headquarters at Eleventh and State, the same building that housed hooker court. His door said "Deputy Chief of Detectives, Field Group A." A job he'd recently been promoted to. McCoo is a big man, broad rather than really tall, with a medium-brown complexion. He had rare gruff moods, more often was businesslike, and this morning seemed almost giddy, which was definitely *not* typical of him. Ordinarily he was friendly and courteous, even generous with his time and advice, but today he verged on the silly.

"Which one is this?" I asked.

"Southern European. They roast the beans much darker and you develop a flavor that's kind of—"

"Burned?"

"Not burned. Deeply roasted aroma. It's an almost meaty aroma. And of course the brew is much darker. People who prefer it consider the other, lighter roasts to be bland and—"

"Feeble?"

"Well, possibly feeble. At least not as robust. But to an evenhanded observer, there's truth in the lighter-roast people's claim that you get more of the taste of the bean in the lighter roast."

"So?"

"So what?"

"So which are you?"

"Oh, my goodness, Cat! Surely you realize that I can see the good in both sides of the argument. I have an urbane, multinational palate, capable of enjoying both the light and the dark, just so long as the bean is flavorful, the grind fresh, and the brew properly made."

"Jeez, McCoo! What's with you today?"

"Susanne got her final report from the pathology people Friday."

"And?"

"Finally, they're sure it's nailed down. There was only one positive lymph node."

"That's great!" For some reason best known to hospital labs, they'd thought at first there'd been five. That would have been bad. For some other reason best known to hospital labs, it had taken them three weeks to decide what the facts were. "All the same, they shouldn't have kept you two stretched out on the rack this long."

"I get angry. I surely do. Then I remember how the lab here in the department works."

"Yeah. It doesn't make it right."

"No, but it keeps me from reaming out the doctor, anyhow."

"Tell Susanne I've been thinking about her."

"I will."

"What's the . . . the situation now?"

"Well, you know. The lumpectomy's healed. She's started radiation and chemo already. But everybody's very—um, very hopeful."

Hopeful can be a terrifying word. "The lump was small, wasn't it? Everything ought to be all right."

"Ought to."

I sat and sipped coffee, not quite sure whether he wanted to talk about Susanne or not. I didn't want to push him. McCoo sometimes wants an ear, sometimes he's in his independent male mode. My ear is always available.

"So what brings you here, Cat?"

"I've got a kind of personal crisis." As his face started to look serious, I quickly said, "No, not bad news. I think it's good news, in fact. But it's scary."

"Tell Uncle Harold."

"Right. After the piece I wrote on the Lottery scandal, I got a lot of attention for a while."

"And well deserved, my dear."

"Will you stop the 'uncle' stuff. You can't be more than seven or eight years older than I am."

"Talk."

"So Channel Three asked me if I would do an investigative report for them now and then."

"Great!"

"So you say. But, McCoo, I'm a print media person. I've never worked in television."

"So write it first, then read it."

"Oh, come on! In the first place, I don't know how I'd sound on the air. Or how I'd look."

"You sound like a normal person and you look okay to me."

"Swell."

"What do they want you to do?"

"I research and write a story. Then they send me a cameraman or whatever they're called these days. And I show him some places and some people and he videotapes them. Some of the people I would interview on camera. Then they flesh out the story, literally, with the interviews, and they cut the tape and paste it and put it together. I sort of, um, narrate. The whole thing is supposed to be maybe five minutes."

"Nothing to it. Obviously all the technical work is going to be taken care of by people who actually know what they're doing."

"Thanks again, McCoo. You're such a morale builder. But it's scary anyway. It's not only that it's completely new to me. It's so *exposed!*"

"Well, that's life, isn't it? I mean life as it ought to be lived."

"What is?"

"Challenging yourself."

"I guess I've said that myself once or twice. But, see, there's another problem besides how you look and sound. There's a big difference between writing and doing this television essay stuff. I work with words. I get the facts, but then I play with the wording. Change the order, poke the thing, and prod it until it takes on a shape."

"So?"

"So what I'm supposed to do here is interview people on videotape. And except for the intro, what I'll wind up with is *their* words, all kinds of things they've said *on tape*."

"It's still words."

"But in chunks, see. It's as if somebody gave me the facts for an article, but in whole paragraphs. And therefore I couldn't really write it. I just had to move the chunks around in big blocks and hope they fit together intelligently."

"Oh. Yeah, I can see how that might be different."

"It's scary."

"Think of it this way. Other people have done it, so probably you can."

I sipped coffee. Well, I could certainly try.

"Cat, are you at some kind of crossroads?"

"Good guess. In a way. Freelance reporting is a funny business. Several of the investigations I've done over the past year or two have been, you know, really high profile. Couple of them developed into major national stories. The murder of Louise Sugarman, chicanery in the Lottery, whatever."

"That's good, isn't it?"

"Yes, but it's strange the way it's worked out. What's happened is that I'm better known—"

"Which is good."

"Which ought to be good, except that the media, especially the daily papers, think I must be more expensive now, so they don't call as much. So I get less work, so I don't make as much money. It's not fair!"

"Can't you tell them? Or maybe just put out the word?"

"Cat Marsala is as cheap as ever? I'm trying that. And word will eventually spread. It's a small world, reporting. But, see, then I ask myself what I'm really working for. I mean, McCoo, I am on the go *all* the time. All the time. If I were in a normal kind of business, I'd have been working up in the company, getting Brownie points for loyalty and for doing a good job, getting maybe a small raise each year. Not in this business, though. Haven't I earned a little more money? When do I get to rest on my laurels?"

He sighed. "It isn't easy. I've seen cops who were everything you could want in an officer. Moving up—sergeant, lieutenant, looking to be a major player some day. And they run afoul of one of the brass, and that's it. They're as high as they'll ever go. Do you like what you do?"

"A lot of the time, McCoo. Quite a lot of the time."

"Then you're okay, really. Aren't you?"

I sipped more coffee. "I guess I am."

"So what do you need from me?" he said.

"Do I always need something?"

"Usually."

"Hey, I've given you stuff, too. I gave you the killer in the Lottery murder."

"True. Let's pretend I owe you one."

"Pretend indeed! Well, this deal I'm working on is about prostitution in Chicago. I need to find some prostitutes. Could you put me in touch with a Vice cop or two?"

"We've got no lack, Catherine. I can tell you that. We've got no lack."

THE EIGHTEENTH DISTRICT Police Station is on Chicago Avenue, about ten blocks west of the lake. Like most east-west streets in Chicago, Chicago Avenue starts ritzy near the lake and then goes through changes. Chicago Avenue itself originates in the heart of the campus of Northwestern University, at the Law School and the Medical School, crosses Michigan Avenue between some of the priciest stores on earth, and then wends its way into a grittier part of town. By the time you get to the Eighteenth District station, nine blocks inland, you are in a mix of deli and hot-dog storefronts, jeans stores, an occasional dry cleaner, thrift shops, and the small upstairs rental offices where podiatrists, fortune-tellers, and tailors hang out.

Aside from special buildings like the Academy, the Chicago Police Department operates two principal kinds of police buildings, the areas and the districts. Districts are what patrol officers work out of. There are twenty-five district stations in Chicago. Areas are what detectives work out of. There are six area headquarters, so naturally each area takes in several districts. Most area headquarters are located in the same building as the most centrally located of the districts they serve.

Vice works out of the districts, but the Vice cops seemed to me to mosey around more than others. And of course, like the detectives, they usually were not in uniform. I'd been told to find Officer Ross Wardon. I asked the desk sergeant whether Wardon was really in the station. She said, "Yeah, he's here someplace. Sit down. I'll find out."

I sat on a blue plastic bench. A highly indignant Hispanic woman dragging a squalling toddler seized the sergeant's attention and started in on a long story about a purse snatcher. Meanwhile the toddler smeared purple lollipop on the back of the woman's yellow dress. I was grateful when the sergeant found an officer to interview the woman, then picked up a phone and called someplace in back. After a couple of minutes she eyeballed me and said, "Hey!"

I jumped up. "Yes?"

"He'll be a few minutes."

"I'll be here." I sat down.

It was now five o'clock in the afternoon. I had had my two o'clock pick-me-up of coffee with Harold McCoo, but I'd walked here afterward, a distance of approximately three miles. I thought of getting some water at the drinking fountain, then I remembered hearing a story about that fountain from a radio news reporter. He'd been waiting for one of the cops to issue a statement on a case he was working. He'd gone to the fountain, but no water came out. Being a reporter, he kicked it. And a zillion roaches came running out of the bottom.

Which didn't mean they were in the water pipes, but it takes the edge off your thirst just the same.

McCoo had made a call to Bob Cleary, Commander at the Eighteenth District, and asked him to put me in touch with an experienced Vice cop. I was about to see what I got.

Ross Wardon was probably either picking up some paper or dropping off some paper or generating some new paper, if I knew my department. Like all bureaucracies, their paper trails could wallpaper all of Chicago. Every week.

Two women police officers clomped past me, escorting a little guy toward the back of the building. Change his outfit and he could be a jockey. Unfortunately, his present outfit consisted entirely of a set of long red underwear. Entirely. No shoes, no hat, nothing. He was saying, "But I really can climb it! Just give me ten minutes and I'll show you. I can climb any building in the world!"

They disappeared down the hall. A different, whiny male voice started at the far end of the hall where they had vanished and came toward me. "Plus, you hadda let me go or else you wouldn'ta, and I know false arrest when I see it. You're gonna hear from my lawyer!" The voice got closer and turned out to be that of a fat white man. He had three chins and his whole face looked greased. He was followed by a uniformed black male cop who was making shooing motions with his hands.

"And when I do there's gonna be a lawsuit like you've never seen, 'n' you waita the city of Chicago pays me a coupla million, then you're gonna ask yourself why you were such a fucking idiot in the first place—" At this point he was passing me by. Thank goodness. "—picking me up when I wasn't doin' nothin' anyhow, no crime just standin' and lookin' at a Cash Station and not doin' anything just lookin' even if it was a long time and all I can say is it better not happen again 'cause I'll sue your ass off—"

He faded out the front door. The cop who had been following him stood in the doorway as if to make sure he was gone, then gave a little flap gesture with his hand, like shaking water off his fingers.

Meanwhile, a racetrack tout type was lurching down the same hall. It was a zoo here. Sloppy clothes, with a mud-brown-and-mustard plaid rumpled jacket. Overweight. Down-at-the-heel shoes. I stood back to let him pass.

"Cat Marsala?" he said.

Oh, jeez. It was my contact.

I looked at him.

He looked at me.

It was caution at first sight.

WE WALKED EAST on Chicago Ave toward Michigan. "The way I get it," Wardon said, "is I tell you about the streets and you buy me dinner."

"You tell me about the streets and you introduce me to some hookers. I need to find women who'll talk for the camera."

"And you buy me dinner."

"And I buy you dinner."

He draped his right arm over my shoulders, which brought his chest up next to mine. His right hand hung down over my right shoulder, the fingers much too far down to be casual. I stopped in the middle of the sidewalk.

"Wardon, this is a professional relationship!"

"What do you mean, professional?"

"You're a cop—"

"And you're a journalist, huh?"

"Reporter, anyway." Journalist sounds so pretentious.

"Listen, good-looking babe like you—"

"Professional. Professional, with a capital 'P' and that rhymes with 'B' and that stands for 'Back off.' And for 'Be your age.'"

But he didn't move his hand. He said, "Come on. I know you don't mean it."

"You right-handed, Ross?"

"Yeah."

"You value that hand?"

"Hey, little girl. I have a gun."

"I have teeth. Do *not* make an issue of this."

"Well!" He removed his hand. "What are you? Sort of pure and all that?"

"Sort of. And it's not your business."

"Then you can't think much of these cunts you're interviewing."

"Wardon, I don't really like that kind of talk. I don't know what makes a woman become a hooker. That's one of the things I want to find out."

"Simple. They want money or drugs and they don't want to work for it."

"It seems to me they not only work, they take risks." By now we were walking along the sidewalk again.

"Yeah, and there's some of 'em are risk junkies. I'll show you a coupla bars, the whores go there when they're not working to hang around gangsters."

"Oh?"

"What's a nice girl like you doing with a topic like this, anyhow? You could find more rewarding people to interview, you look around a little."

"Hey. I got assigned this topic. This is what I get paid for." I studied him from the side. "You're kidding me, aren't you? Spin me around a few times, see if you can mix me up? You really aren't as insensitive as you're trying to appear. You couldn't be, hanging around these women all the time, you've got to see how sad a lot of them are."

"Wrong. This is me. What you see is what you get."

We walked down Rush Street, which is an area of tourist clubs, not that some natives don't go there, too, but out-of-towners are always told about it in hotel booklets of the "Chicago After Dark" type and by concierges and taxi drivers. It was now six o'clock on Tuesday night.

"I suppose Saturday nights are the big nights for hookers," I said.

"Street hookers, yes. Escort services, no. The high-end escort services do zip on Saturday. The traveling businessmen are back in their cozy homes, and diplomats and state visitors and all that kind of thing have functions to go to. Saturday nights are nights off for the high-priced spread."

"The high-priced—oh." Good Lord! This guy was Piltdown Man reborn in Illinois. Why did they ever assign me this turkey? However, this was not the place or time to make a problem of it. "Okay. What are the busy hours? Evening? Late night?"

"Nope. There's a flurry of business between four and six P.M. Even for street hookers. Men on their way home. It's sorta like stopping by the bar for one for the road before heading back to the wife and screaming kiddies. Then business drops off until after ten. Especially escorts that go to hotels. The visiting businessmen are at dinner. Midnight's big. There again, the top end of the pay scale is different. Doesn't start until late. A guy who makes millions usually is also a guy who works late."

We were walking along Rush when Wardon said, "Hey, come on in here."

He ducked into a club. It was not a particularly dirty place, and while the sign in front had photographs of some well-nourished women, to my eye it looked like the entertainment would be fairly bland. The guy standing by the inner door wearing a tux and a razor-thin mustache blinked at Wardon but didn't do anything like shout a code word for "cop" or push a panic button. As far as I could tell.

There was a stage show going on, bathed in a blue spotlight. A woman in silvery sequins was dancing to very loud music between two guys who seemed to be pulling off little patches of the sequins. I wondered what she stuck them on with. Glue-stick? To make this work she would have to have shaved off every body hair first, or she'd be yelping all the time.

While I was making these observations, Wardon was heading over to a stair, and seeing me daydreaming, he grabbed my hand and pulled me after him.

Halfway upstairs, the music was less loud, and he said, "You gotta stay with me."

"Why? This doesn't look like a dangerous place."

"Just do what I say."

The stairway opened onto a landing with a metal door. Oh ho, I thought. Wardon pounded on it. A peek-grille opened and an eyeball studied Wardon. The door opened.

A man who looked too small to be a bouncer stepped back and let us in.

We were in a room that was almost a duplicate of the one below. Except that there was no dancer. There was a blue light, some music playing—the same music as downstairs, but not as loud. There were drum-sized glossy black tables all over the room, about half of them occupied. Then I noticed that the dancer from downstairs was gyrating on a large television screen placed near the ceiling and angled slightly downward. The customers were idly watching and drinking. Some were eating.

As we entered, every eye turned to fix on Wardon and me.

He went to an empty table, pulled out a chair for himself, and said "Sit down" to me.

"What is this?" I asked.

"Just a minute. Two bourbons," he told the waiter. The customers stopped staring at us. But they still knew we were here.

The women in the room were mostly gorgeous. And they wore clothes that cost about as much as two months' rent for my apartment. I'm no expert in men's suits, but these fitted; Ross was far and away the worst-dressed male in the room. Some of the tables held women sitting together, but most were mixes of men and women, not always in pairs. There were a couple of tables of men, talking vehemently to each other. My mind came up with any number of hypotheses before Wardon said, "This ain't no bust-out bar, you know."

"What's a bust-out bar?"

He produced a pitying grimace. But he loved my ignorance. "Oh, you know. Cheap trick place. Girls giving hand jobs under the tablecloth. Like that."

Right. "So what is this?"

"This is sort of a staging area."

"What for?"

"For the evening. The women are mostly call girls. But some of them are *really* top of the line. No calls. Recommendation only."

"And the men are what? Johns? Their customers?"

"Mob guys."

"Mob guys? Why? What's—you mean mob guys who run these women? Pimps?"

"Mostly no. This is like neighborhood to them. It's a place where they can all rest up, you might say. Be themselves. Or could if we weren't here, of course, heh-heh-heh!" He chuckled happily into his bourbon.

"What do you mean, rest?"

"See, what is it? Six? Six-thirty?" He was wearing a watch but he was too lazy to look at it.

"Six-thirty."

"This is a slow period for the girls. Customers are at dinner or whatever. Plus, the girls are basically just getting up. This is like the equivalent of maybe nine-thirty in the morning for a citizen. The girls are here after maybe an hour of work and the mob guys are just kind of getting up. Call this mid-morning coffee."

"So, the women come in here to wait for later in the evening?"

"Yeah. But not entirely. Lotta these hookers get off on being around power. They're power junkies. Power groupies, you might say. They like to go with corporation heads, CEO types, or mob guys. They loooooove to hang around mob guys. And the guys themselves like to have these good-looking broads draped all over the place. They like to have them around, but at the same time mostly they ignore them. Look at 'em. The guys are mostly doing business with each other."

It was true. I'd already noticed it.

I said, "And they know who you are."

"Oh, sure. The chickens know the fox."

"But they're not throwing you out."

"Why make a scene? They know I'll go away after a while. They're not going to do anything really exciting while I'm here."

"Anything like what?"

"See the guy with the little gold spoon on the chain around his neck?"

"Hey. I know a coke spoon when I see one."

"Oh, we're not tally naive, are we? Okay. See the woman with the purple fingernails? Next to the fat guy? She's kind of dancing around from table to table?"

"Yeah?"

"See the one fingernail that's longer than the others?"

"Yeah."

"That's her coke finger. Scoop it up in one long fingernail."

"Oh."

"See the other woman, sitting at the table blowing smoke rings and putting her finger through them?"

"Yeah?"

"She's not on crack or coke. What else, I don't know."

"How do you know that?"

"If they're sitting still, they're not on coke. Anyway, they'll hold off on powdering their noses while we're here. They're just *dying* for us to leave." He laughed some more.

I studied the crowd, plugging in all this stuff in my mind.

"These professional women, the type you got here are mostly on coke," Ross said, "not crack. This group, crack kind of marks you as lower class. The *less* expensive hookers do crack, mostly. These aren't your street hookers. They're more your call girls. Now, a lotta places this time of the evening you'd have your B-girls out in force."

"What are B-girls?"

"Bar girls. Hang around bars to get picked up and taken to a room and laid, basically. But not here. Because here they don't need 'em."

"Why'd you bring me here, Wardon?"

"I want you to be realistic."

"About what?"

"You're gonna sentimentalize these hookers. I can see it in your eyes. And you'd be wrong. These are hard women. They're living the fast life—great clothes, best booze, best restaurants, best drugs, and they're getting the kind of excitement they love."

"They're killing themselves."

"Maybe. But not right away. And listen—they're vicious. They'd knock you down and stab you to death with their spike heels if they could see money in it for them."

"Okay. You've made your point."

"In that case, let's get out of here. There's a thousand more stories in the naked city." He drained his bourbon. "I assume you're paying."

I paid.

FOUR

WE MOSEYED ALONG Rush Street northward for a while, then took a turn east.

"In this district, you got the richest and the poorest people in Chicago, all in the one district. You got the fanciest restaurants, hundred bucks an ounce of anything, and you got places mix horse in their hamburgers and that's not the worst thing they do. Now, six blocks that way, you got Holy Name Cathedral." He pointed south. "Two blocks that way," he said pointing west, "you got storefront whorehouses, and in the back they sell little boys or rent 'em out by the week or month. Four blocks that way"—he pointed northwest—"you got Cabrini Green, and some of the poorest people in the United States. Four blocks that way"—Ross pointed southeast—"you got these new condos on Michigan Ave, they start at a million-two for one bedroom. And they're *walking distance*."

I didn't quite know what he was getting at, so I waited.

"You want to see every kind of hooker known to man, you got it right here. But you watch yourself. You can go from safe to dangerous in a block, so you watch your ass."

We kept walking east. He was right about this being a quick-change neighborhood. In the distance of one building, we had gone from a commercial area with trendy shops and nightclubs to a residential neighborhood with large trees and huge houses. From their architecture, most of the houses had been built in the late 1800s.

"Nice-looking street here, huh? This one?"

"Yes, it is."

"Lotta houses here."

"Houses, obviously—oh, you mean as in whore-house?"

"That's it. This is expensive country right around here. Some top-quality houses. Extremely expensive girls. Diplomatic contacts. All that kind of thing."

"Diplomatic as in foreign consulates?"

"Oh, yeah. They kind of expect it, foreigners, people tell me. As a matter fact, in most European countries these places are pretty open. And escort services, too. Men exchange gossip on all the latest girls."

"Not here, though?"

"No. In the U S of A men are kind of embarrassed to admit that they have to pay for sex. Howsomever, you got your consulates here, you got your multinational corporations, and I can tell you *they* know where the best houses are."

We were passing some beautiful old buildings, gray or white or brown stone with wrought-iron gates and leaded-glass windows. Most were three or four stories. One was reddish stone with a lighted octagonal cupola on top of the third floor. Another had been built by a playful giant with blocks of granite the size of Toyotas. The lawns were well landscaped, but small because this was still a city street and space was at a premium. Most seemed to be single-family houses; one even had a tri-cycle on the lawn, and I wondered if Ross knew what he was talking about. But several had three name-plaques on the front and three doorbells, one for each floor. These were polished-brass name-plaques. Nothing but the best. It meant multiple occupancy, but that didn't mean whorehouses.

Then an absolutely drop-dead gorgeous woman got out of a taxi that had pulled to the curb ahead of us. She had legs so long you wondered how she got in the cab in the first place, and eyelashes so long you could have braided them. Her skirt was mid-length but slit as high as a sarong, and her fingernails had not washed dishes in many a long year. And her hair was the color of the setting sun.

"Wow," I said.

"My, my!"

She paid the cabdriver, whose facial expression of intense longing suggested there were other ways she could pay him, and walked up the stone steps to a house that had only one doorbell. She pushed the bell. The door opened.

The woman who opened the door was equally lovely, but with straight black hair, and she was wearing a much lower neckline.

Meanwhile, a stunning black woman with a cloud of curly hair and a small delicate face drifted past the window on the right. The door closed.

Ross said, "See?"

"Yes."

"Two, three thousand bucks a night, easy."

"Really?"

"More, some places. Plus, any way you want it. You want the woman dressed like a French maid—little black dress, white lace cap, little tiny white apron? No problem. Dressed like a tiger? Body paint, stripes, long nails? No problem. Cost you, but no problem."

"Oh." After a few seconds I asked the typical suburbanite's question. "Don't the neighbors complain?"

"Well, that's the wicked city for you. Matter of fact, sometimes they do complain. But look at the place. It's well kept, the lawn's mowed, the windows are washed, the inhabitants are quiet, you can bet they soundproof the walls, and the taxes are paid on time. Suppose the neighbors complain and the next tenant is some guy with a zillion teenagers playing boom boxes all night? Is that an improvement?"

"I see what you mean."

"Plus, these people just might have an occasional in with an alderman."

"A payoff?"

"That or favors. Visiting fireman in town, who knows? They have their problems, though. These houses."

"Such as?"

"Burglary. See, if they get robbed, they don't dare call the police."

"Oh."

"These here are pretty expensive places. They maybe even own the whole building, got their own security system, but your average down-market whorehouse is seriously exposed to burglary. It's usually the first floor of a building, and they like to be in buildings that don't have doormen."

"For obvious reasons." I was writing in my notebook.

"For obvious reasons. So they're not especially well protected from theft."

"Okay."

"Then there's extortion."

"Extortion by who?"

"The mob, of course. See, a lotta people think your mob runs prostitution and gambling and such."

"They don't?"

"No. Not like in the sense of setting them up. Sometimes, but not usually. See, what happens with your illegal business is the mob comes around and offers protection."

"Protection from themselves."

"Sure. Like we won't break your windows or your legs if you pay us. Happens in every illegal business—chop shops, bookies, whorehouses. The mob skims a cut."

"And the houses can't complain."

"Can't hardly go to the police like an honest businessman would, now can they?"

Another breathtakingly beautiful woman got out of a cab.

"Hey, Ross?" I said. "Do you think she'd give me an interview?"

"She'd give you three guys with scar tissue over their eyes." He laughed. "Still—"

"Still what?"

"We did have a little problem at one a these places a couple months ago. One a their girls got a little high and started shooting at the neighbor's wall. We calmed everybody down. Didn't arrest her. Maybe they figure they owe me one."

"Really? Could you get me an introduction?" A seriously expensive hooker was going to be almost impossible for me to get, otherwise, and I wanted one. I was not yet sure how I wanted to design the TV essay, but I was starting to think it would be good to have the full range of prostitutes.

"Maybe. Maybe. Let me think about it."

"You get these people in debt to you, Ross?"

"Yeah. Once in a while they do favors."

"What are you talking about now? Sexual favors?"

He didn't know me well, and I was a reporter, and he was cautious. But he was also disgustingly proud of himself. He said, "Well, after all, they're hookers."

"So?"

"They're not the same as women like you, Marsala. If they gave a person a little something, they wouldn't really be giving away anything they really valued, would they?"

There were things I could say about holding the law over these women and then extracting sex from them. But not now. Plus I wasn't entirely sure Ross wasn't making fun of me, seeing if I'd buy his story. Seeing if he could get a rise out of me. I didn't have Ross pegged yet.

He took a turn south on Michigan Avenue. I trailed along in his wake. For a few blocks we had the Drive and Lake Michigan on our left. Then we passed the Drake Hotel and plunged from the high-rent district into the extremely high-rent district. We sauntered past Bloomingdale's, Tiffany, Ciro, Brooks Brothers, and Cartier, at the same time passing one world-class hotel after another. Hidden away in one arcade of shops, its window for some reason a riot of artificial spring flowers, was Condom Gallere. Obviously a sign of the times. We crossed the Chicago River, which flows backward, from Lake Michigan toward the Mississippi. This is just as well for the health of Lake Michigan. In the old days all the sewage from the city of Chicago went into the river and then flowed straight out into Lake Michigan and spread out onto the beaches. Chicago history buffs say that in order to make it flow backward, engineers moved more tons of earth than was moved in digging the Panama Canal.

People in furs, people in Levi's, panhandlers, uniforms, people of all colors and shapes and sizes flowed by as we walked south. And every once in a while—maybe once out of every fifty or sixty people—Ross would cock his head toward a woman and say to me, "Hooker." A little time would pass and he'd say again, "Hooker."

Again. "Hooker."

After a while I couldn't stand it any longer.

"Ross, you don't really know whether a woman is a hooker or not. You're just trying to impress me."

"Hey, babe. I know my business."

"Okay. How do you know those were prostitutes?"

"Of the last ten, seven I've arrested or seen at the station."

"Oh. That's not fair. And the other three?"

"Well, hey. Years of experience."

"You're full of it, Ross."

"Oh? Let's follow one."

"Sure, sure. Show me. One you haven't arrested before."

We sauntered on down Michigan, blending as well as anybody else into one of the most multigenerational, multiethnic, multi-income crowds on earth. It was only a block before Ross said, "There."

"Who?"

"The one with the big red purse."

She looked to me like a lot of other women. Although, as we walked along twenty feet behind her, I noticed some similarities to the other women Ross had pointed out. She was very carefully dressed. Not especially flashy, but every detail was in place. So what? That applied to a lot of women. Not me, unfortunately, but a lot. Careful makeup, too. Other than that, what? Well, she carried a large purse. So had the other women he had pointed out.

She strode another half block farther, then turned into the Hotel Stratford, one of the more discreet pleasure domes along this stretch. We followed. The Stratford was as expensive as the others, maybe more so, with polished brass floor tiles and walls of alternating smoky mirrors and brushed copper. Chandeliers hung from high ceilings.

The woman crossed directly to the elevators.

"She's just a guest going to her room, Ross."

"No, she's going to somebody else's room."

"She's come back from dinner or something—"

We were now close enough so that when a tiny sound came from her purse, I could hear it. She stopped and reached in instantly to turn it off. We kept walking, hoping she wouldn't notice us staring, but I saw her take a beeper from her purse and look at the phone number it displayed. Meanwhile, Ross was saying to me, "Wait! I gotta call the office."

"Now?"

He hurried to the bank of phones and then I understood why. He got to the phones before she did, and he had dialed before she arrived, so it didn't look like we were following her.

"Hey, Mike!" he said. "Why'd you call?"

Faintly, I could hear the ringing sound on the other end of his line. He wasn't actually talking to anybody. He probably called his own home phone.

The woman got whoever it was she was calling. I could not hear anything. She was too far away. But she took out a small notebook and made some notes. Then she hung up and went to the elevators. Ross went on talking to himself until the elevator doors opened and she entered.

"See?"

"Oh, all right. I suppose she was getting her next assignment from her service."

"You suppose right."

"She *could* be an out-of-town executive being beeped to call back the home office."

"Oh, yeah? And why didn't she wait to call back in the relaxing privacy of her own hotel room, then?"

"An emergency? No. Okay, okay."

We went back out through the revolving brushed-brass doors and onto Michigan Avenue. "Why do they carry big purses, Ross?"

"Gear. Some extra clothes in case theirs get ripped. Street hookers, you know, usually have a stash of clothes someplace, under a garbage can or some such. Of course, in these fancy hotels what you're seeing is your moderately to seriously expensive escort-service girls."

"So?"

"So they have to carry clothes plus that gadget that you use to stamp credit cards."

"Credit cards! They take charges?"

"Sure. Your streetwalker, now, she takes cash. Only. But these ladies accept credit cards."

"All right. Let *me* try."

"Be my guest."

We strolled along Michigan, and at the Lawrencia, the next hotel, I saw a woman alone, carrying a large blueberry-blue bag. She had glossy hair, long lithe legs, and glittery clothes, and from the back she looked like exactly what I was looking for. "That one. Let's catch up," I said.

She slowed to go in the revolving doors, and I caught up too quickly. She glanced back, feeling followed.

"Sandra!"

"Cat!" She took one look at Ross and pushed inside the revolving door. Inside, she started walking away. I followed.

"Wait a second!"

"Cat, that man is a cop!"

"He's not here to bother you. Ross, can you wait in the bar?"

"Sure, babe."

"Were you following me?" Sandra asked.

"How could I follow you? I don't know where you've been."

"Listen, I've got an appointment."

She looked entirely different. Her hair was washed and styled, and its warm, chestnut red-brown was dynamite against a powder-blue dress shot with silvery threads. The dress buttoned up the front. While the neckline was not really low, the top two buttons were undone, and I could imagine a man wanting to follow where the trail of buttons led. With her lips a glossy pink, face made up, and ready to party, this was no longer Waif Sandra. Her head was high, one hand on her hip. This was Sophisticated Sandra. Seductive Sandra. She carried a playbill. I glanced at it. It was for a play that had closed several weeks before.

"I just happened to see you," I said, half lying. "Will you call me sometime?"

"Maybe. I'm thinking about it."

"Well, okay."

"See you."

"Uh, Sandra?"

"Yeah?"

"Do you carry one of those things that stamps credit cards?"

She cocked her head, smiled, and said, "Sure."

I PICKED ROSS UP in the bar, waited while he finished a beer, and paid for him. Ross then guided me through three upper Michigan Avenue hotel bars, pointing out B-girls. This was quite easy. You see a woman sitting alone at a bar in a short skirt with her legs crossed, watching in the bar mirror for good prospects, you can guess what she's doing. I tried to talk to one, a black woman of about twenty-three, who was smiling gently at the bartender. But when I started, "I'm a television reporter—" she said, "Move your ass, honey, you're blocking my light."

Back on the street again, I said, "Ross, I need one of them. I want to meet a top-of-the-line hooker who's willing to talk with me."

"I'll think about it."

"You have to think *fast*. I don't have long to get this show together."

"Mmmm."

He steered me to a couple of street corners near seedy drugstores—and yes, only a block and a half from the Gold Coast hotels—where "working women" hung around the front doors. One corner was so busy with cars slowing down to pick up women, traffic was backed up into the streets that fed into it.

Ross said, "We call that a 'John jam.'"

It's all in knowing where to look.

Ross said, "See, your basic hooker has a territory. If she's a streetwalker, it might be only half of one block, on one side of the street. Some places, she crosses the street, the girl on the other side stabs her."

"Stabs her?"

"Or her pimp does. Same thing. I mean, they *own* their territory. They'll fight for it."

Ever since I saw Sandra, I'd been wanting to ask something. "Ross, I was thinking. It seemed like such a coincidence when I ran into Sandra, but I realized that was the hotel where she was arrested last week. The cop mentioned it."

"So?"

"Does she go there because she's got a territory, too? Is that her, uh, stroll?"

"Call girls and these escort-service people aren't so territorial. No, the service probably has a contact."

"What do you mean?"

"Like the concierge, for instance. Somebody in the hotel steers them business."

"How?"

"A man who's staying there goes to the doorman or the concierge or whatever and just asks how to get a girl for the evening. And the steerer tells him."

"What's in it for the concierge?"

"You kiddin'?"

Okay. Payback. Probably the guy is on some sort of retainer. In this case from Beau Monde.

"Ross, if hookers are so territorial, do you mean if you've picked up one before, you can just go back tonight and find her in the same place again?"

"More'n likely. If she's a street hooker. It's not just that a Loop hooker isn't gonna be on West Belmont, or a Sixty-third Street hooker on Rush, or a Belmont Street hooker on Sixty-third Street. You could go to Division, which I often do, and you know which girls are gonna be between 100 East and 50 East. And they're completely different from the crowd at 100 West, and *they're* not the same as the gang at 200 West."

"If the cops wanted to arrest an escort like Sandra, how would they do it?"

"Probably call the escort service, ask for a girl. Ask to hire a girl to go out on the town. She offers sex for money—he's got her."

"That's entrapment!"

"No. Not if she offers."

"Do you do that? Arrest them like that?"

"Used to."

"Not anymore?"

"Me, not so much. It's not entrapment, but it's too much like shooting fish in a barrel."

He stopped and stretched, his big stomach bulging out over a black leather belt.

He said, "Well, let's go eat."

"Just like that? Suddenly it's time to feed you?"

"That's the deal, isn't it? The brass wants me to show you around. But they can't tell me what to do when I'm not on duty. Why do you think I'm going to all this trouble, tell you all this neat stuff, hang around with you?"

"You sure are a flatterer, Ross."

"Hey! I could be home with a beer. I could be putting my feet up—"

"No, no, don't explain. I realize you have your own life to live. And I appreciate your help. I certainly intend to keep my part of the bargain. How about this?" I gestured at Ristorante Mario.

"Hey, none of that wop food. It's all flour."

"Oh, really? Chicken cacciatore is flour?" No answer. I sighed. We walked another half block. "How about this?" Szechwan Village was one of the best restaurants in Chicago, and not one that would bleed my TV expense allowance dry.

"None of that chink stuff, either. It's all vegetables."

I shuddered to think what he'd say if I suggested Vietnamese, Thai, Polish, soul, or any of the other hundred restaurants around here. However, it was not my job to reform Ross, a reminder I seemed to be making to myself a lot—and besides, I still thought he was intentionally trying to get my goat. I sighed loudly enough for him to hear it and folded my arms. "All right. *What*, then?"

"Corner." He pointed.

Sure enough, on the next corner on our side of the street was the entrance to a restaurant inside a towering new hotel. It was called The Cattleman's Chuck Wagon.

"Fine," I said. I didn't have the heart to tell him that the hotel was Japanese owned.

IT WAS NOT VERY LATE when I got home, only nine-thirty, but I knew as I opened the door that Long John Silver would be angry. Long John, whom I call LJ, is my parrot.

LJ is an African gray parrot. These are not the flamboyant red-and-yellow or blue-and-green Amazon parrots everybody is so fond of. African grays are a drab, dull gunmetal color with patches of a dry-blood red on their lower bodies and tails.

But can they ever talk!

I'm always careful to tell people that LJ would not be here, or be owned by me, if he had not been brought to the United States before I was born. In that sense he's a politically correct parrot. I'm not in favor of trapping wild tropical birds, especially parrots, and shipping them to the United States. They reproduce slowly enough in the wild, and the populations aren't replacing themselves. Also, a majority of the birds caught die either in being caught or in being transported.

I'm not even much in favor of breeding parrots in captivity, unless there's a way of being sure they're going to good homes—and how can you ever be sure? But I have to admit that breeding programs at least take the pressure off trapping wild birds, and they keep the gene pool going.

LJ belonged many years ago to the captain of a Louisiana shrimp trawler. He was passed along to a Creole chef who came up the Mississippi to Chicago and opened a restaurant. The chef died suddenly, and LJ was adopted by an English professor who lived in my building. The professor owned LJ for twenty years before he got involved in a nasty escapade with a woman—the professor, not LJ—and left in a hurry for Alberta.

Leaving me holding the parrot.

I think LJ is about forty years old, which makes him barely middle-aged, in African gray parrot years. Human years, too, come to think of it.

LJ's long tenure with the English professor left him with a strange and often annoying vocabulary. I never open the apartment door without expecting him to come swooping down shrieking "Call me Ishmael!" or some such, although he prefers Shakespeare.

Today, however, I opened the door and he yelled, *"Braak! Gaaaaah!"*

"All right." I dropped my jacket and stuff at the door. "What did I do now?"

"Braak! Caaawwww!"

He gets incoherent when he's really mad. I started to check. "Food in your food dish. Water in your water dish and more in your bottle. It can't be just that I'm a little late, can it?"

I had come in the back door. But my apartment is very small, shorter, for instance, than your average-sized Chicago bus. So as soon as LJ stopped squawking I could hear a sound from the living room. Cautiously, I peeked around the door.

I had accidentally left the television set on low when I went out in the morning. "Well, no wonder you're mad! Couldn't talk to yourself without interruption, huh?"

LJ said, *"Braaak!"*

"Horrible day, I guess, huh?"

LJ said, *"Gaaah!"*

"Had to watch those game shows all the time, poor baby?"

LJ said, "It was the best of times, it was the worst of times."

"Come on, you and I both know you don't understand what you're saying." African grays are extremely smart, and they can be taught elaborate routines. But they're not *that* smart. They just repeat phrases they've heard. Or pick up on a word you've just said.

I sat down at the word processor to convert my day's and evening's notes to something that I would be able to understand a week from now. If you're working fast on a story and don't do this, you come along later to look for what the mayor, for example, said, and you wonder why he told you "Bks fm suspin di snupf."

The monitor screen lit up. LJ swooped down, landed on my shoulder, and said, "What light from yonder window breaks?"

"Oh, please. Go eat birdseed."

After half an hour I had most of the squiggles converted to bytes. Fortunately, I didn't need to make dinner. Steak, home fries, and apple pie with Ross had been more than I usually eat. So often I get home and find myself confronted with an interesting gastronomic puzzle, like what can be made of limp celery, a little lettuce just turning brown, and a can of refried beans. Answer: a very bad mock-taco salad.

I was just closing the old keyboard and thinking of a long night's rest when the door buzzer buzzed.

Never, never buzz anybody in without looking. Unfortunately, our landlord is too stingy to buy an intercom. Fortunately, I can see down to the glass-window front door from my stairwell.

"John! Come on up."

John Banks is my significant other. He's become more significant in the last few weeks, because I've given up on Mike. Mike is a wonderful person, but I simply can't count on him ever getting anywhere when he says he will. Most of the time he's all right, and then once in a while, when you're depending on him most, he'll go off on an alcoholic bender. And it wasn't helping him that I kept making excuses.

It wasn't helping me, either. I would be furious when he stood me up, lost in a fuzzy stupor in a bar somewhere. Then guilt would flood over me for being judgmental when, after all, he was suffering from an illness. But being whipsawed by emotion left me limp a lot of the time and made it impossible for me to work. My work is important to me.

Do I have guilt about shoving Mike away? There isn't a day that I don't wonder whether I did the right thing. There isn't a night I don't wonder if he's lying in a gutter somewhere freezing to death or being mugged.

Plus John is stable, has a money-making job and a family with money. I don't want to feel like I've copped out. Which isn't John's fault, after all.

I said, "Hi! I was just starting to close down the day—"

"Hiya. And good evening, LJ." John was always meticulous about greeting the bird, and LJ took shameless advantage. Now he perched on John's shoulder and rubbed his beak against John's ear. John pulled something from his pocket.

"Parsley?"

"Not just plain parsley. Italian flat-leaf parsley. For LJ."

"It doesn't have any insecticide, does it?"

"Please! I know better. This is from La Pêche d'Or. They grow their own herbs, you know."

"Forty-dollar parsley, I presume?" La Pêche d'Or was one of the priciest restaurants in Chicago.

"No. I stole it from my mother's plate."

John's mother is intensely particular about people. This is another way of saying she's in the running for the snob-of-the-year award, and a definite contender for snob of the century. She thinks of me as a little like poison ivy—deeply rooted, but capable of being eradicated by constant chopping.

LJ ate the parsley and stayed on John's shoulder. Fickle beast. I was really tired, and John noticed my droopy eyelids.

"How exhausted are you?"

"Why?"

He whipped a package out from under his arm.

"I have the laser disc of *Fantasia.*"

"Oh, my! Oh, golly!"

"Just released today."

"Ooooo." John knows that Disney movies and chocolate are the quickest way to my heart. "I guess I wasn't really *that* tired. Actually, I'm feeling wide awake."

He put the disk in the player and we settled onto the sofa in harmony. I noticed it was 9:58. "Five minutes of the news first?"

"Okay by me," he said. John was really easy to get along with.

Channel Three, which I was coming to think of as my channel, led into the news with music that was halfway between a triumphal march and a pep rally. Then we zoomed in on the anchorpersons, Linda Martinez and Greg Walton. They were good-looking people, which is no surprise, but their outstanding "look" was firm-jawed trustworthiness. These people could tell it to you like it *is*.

"Another battle today in the long-playing City Council wars," Martinez said, "took place when seven councilmen brought debate on the nomination of a director to the teachers' retirement fund to a halt, insisting that an immediate decision be made on the previously tabled streetwalker bill. Channel Three's Diane Fire has the story."

Shot one: File tape of the council chamber, tiers of seats rising away in a crescent shape. Shot two: Video of seven men in the hall outside, an ethnic mix, all wearing three-piece navy suits and shouting at somebody off-camera. Diane Fire with microphone: "The debate about streetwalkers erupted again today when Alderman Fred Holder, Clint "Corky" Alvarado, Bennett Perkins, Lon Smith, Gene Cirincione, Barry Pintakowski, and Mustafa Pa accused the council of sitting on their bill."

Microphone held in front of Pintakowski. "Alderman, what is your argument here?"

"This is an urgent matter! Street hookers lower the tone of our city. Besides which, their presence encourages other crime in the area. And the mayor's just sitting on his—"

"Alderman Pa?"

"Nobody wants hookers around. They hang around near my store, make the customers go someplace else. I run a nice grocery. The mayor is dragging his feet on this."

Fade to Diane Fire, standing on north Michigan Avenue. A man in a brown tweedy suit stands near her. "Jerrold Howard, an alderman known for his liberal views, has doubts."

Howard: "It's not that anybody is in favor of streetwalkers, Diane. It's just that, in a democracy, I think we have to be careful of ordering people off the streets simply because we don't like what they're doing."

"Is the mayor really dragging his feet on this?"

"I'm not privy to the mayor's thoughts."

Diane alone, camera closing in: "Streetwalkers are not confined to any specific part of the city or any income level. And no matter where you go, residents are likely to say, 'Get them off *my* street.' The Pintakowski-Pa-Holder-Alvarado-Perkins-Smith-Cirincione coalition, sometimes called the Sinless Seven, is likely to find considerable support in days to come. Linda?"

"Thank you, Diane—"

I cut the sound down with my remote, a gift from John on the occasion of my moving back into my apartment after a recent fire.

"That's the debate that triggered my assignment," I said. "Three wants an essay on prostitution in general in Chicago."

"An essay such as what?"

"Well, what it is, how much there is, why it is."

"How can you answer why it is?"

"Can't. Not beyond the obvious. Three wants something tear-jerking or infuriating. Like tough women insulting the cameraman. I need to structure the piece my way. Something fresh, though, and that isn't easy. What I can start with is profiles of a few of the women involved."

"So you're planning to interview hookers?"

"Of course. I've got some preliminary feelers out." After an initial resistance early in our relationship, John has been okay about my work. He doesn't always like it, and he becomes very closed up when he thinks it's dangerous, but he's decided that's the job I'm going to do. At least I hope he's decided that.

"Don't you find it upsetting?"

"Well, sure. It's unsettling that these women think that's all their lives are good for."

"I meant—don't you find the topic kind of disgusting."

"What do you mean?"

"Well, at some level, you have to think about what they actually *do*."

"Yes. But there's also why they do it."

"But still, the bottom line is that they've put themselves outside society's values."

"John, it's not enough to say they're terrible people and dismiss them. They're human beings, and it's just not *good enough*. They must have reasons in their childhoods for thinking their lives aren't worth anything better."

"That wasn't what I said. That they're terrible people."

"Well—'outside society's values'—it certainly sounds like you think they're fallen women."

"I'm not a complete troglodyte, Cat!"

"Well, what *do* you think of them?"

"Look, I agree with you. Somebody pretty thoroughly abused them when they were children. Diminished them somehow."

That was better. "But still, John, to just say that—that sounds very superficial. It's like headlines. 'Victim of child abuse.' They have a 'deficient self-image.' But tell me in real, personal terms; suppose you met some of them. What would you really think of them? As people?"

"I'm...not sure."

"Could you love one of them?"

"Cat! I wouldn't go to a hooker!"

"That's not what I'm asking. Could you love one of them as a sister?"

He looked away from me. "I just don't know."

Should I press him to answer? Should I force the issue? Who ever knows what's best when things like this happen between friends?

"John, are you happy?"

He looked puzzled, and frankly I wasn't sure why I wanted to know this right now. But he was just so *accepting* of his life, it frustrated me. It seemed both dull and, unfortunately, smug.

"Well, Cat, I wish you would think about you and me—"

"No, I don't mean our relationship. I mean, what about your job?"

"My *job!* It makes good money. And no heavy lifting." He grinned.

"But do you *like* it? Do you see yourself doing it thirty years from now?"

"It's hard for me to see anything thirty years ahead."

"John, please—"

"All right. All right. I know what you're asking. How much satisfaction can I get, playing the stock market all day for other people?"

"Right."

"Well, you know, it's exciting. Really. It's the world's biggest Monopoly game, and tremendously competitive. You can get addicted to the excitement. It's Monopoly with real money."

"And real scorekeeping. I can see that. But do you feel like you have any—this is going to sound goofy, but do you feel you're doing anything for the good of mankind?"

"Whooo." He leaned back. "No, I suppose not. If I'm going to make a difference in the world, I'd have to do it through charities or maybe political parties."

"Doesn't that bother you?"

"Cat, most jobs don't make much difference to the welfare of mankind. Probably the one job that really makes a difference is grade school teacher, and I'm not the type."

We put on *Fantasia,* and it was wonderful. We watched dancing mushrooms and munched on potato chips and were happy. But underneath I was troubled about John's attitude. He was being honest; he really didn't know whether he could accept a prostitute as a human being, a human being exactly like the rest of us.

FIVE

SHE WAS LONG AND LEAN and tawny, and when she crossed her legs her silk stockings made a *slish-swee!* sound that would drive men wild. Me, I found it slightly annoying.

Felipe, manning the camera, held steady enough, but after all, the camera was on a tripod. I intended to ask him in private later whether his constant deep sighs were really professional behavior.

How did I know the woman's stockings were silk, not nylon? I didn't. I deduced it from her other accessories, the buttery-soft and butter-yellow angora sweater, the pricey wool skirt in a deeper shade of butterscotch yellow, and the toast-brown kid shoes, a pair of which I had seen in a window at Water Tower Place retailing at five hundred and ninety dollars the copy.

The most amazing part of this wardrobe was the gold domino mask she wore. It was just like a burglar's mask in comic books, but was made of a metallic, matte-finished gold fabric. We'd offered her a silhouette interview, or one of those scramblers that make the face look like a mosaic of dancing squares. Neither one appealed to her.

She was going to be anonymous; oh, yes, she had insisted on it when Ross set up the interview. But even if the people who saw her didn't know who she was, she was still going to be gorgeous. She had signed the studio's release form with a flourish, including a sinuous scroll under her name.

"Now, Ms. Leleina," I said, "let me explain how we do this. When the television viewers see the program, they'll first see a short introduction by me, and then we'll go directly to you and some other women talking about their work. So, they won't hear me asking the questions I'm going to ask you now. You see?"

"I see, honey. Go ahead."

"So, what you have to do is give me a complete answer. Okay?"

"Sure, honey." She crossed her legs into a more delectable position. Felipe sighed. I went on.

"Okay. Ms. Leleina, what line of work are you in?"

"Entertainment."

"Fine, but see, if the viewer just hears that, he doesn't know what it's about. You need to say something like, 'I'm in the entertainment business.'"

"I'm in the entertainment business."

"Um, okay. Now, how do you find your clients?"

"Referral, honey."

"Well, see, Ms. Leleina, you can't talk to *me*. And I need a complete sort of answer, that kind of tells a story, like, 'My clients hear about me from other men who—'"

We went on like this for close to twenty minutes. What broke the logjam was not that she really got the idea. Ms. Dominique Leleina was not terribly verbal in an abstract way. But she was verbal in a personal way. What happened was that she relaxed and started to talk. Her voice was sweet, soft, low, gentle, not with any southern drawl, but with a hint of the philosophy behind the southern drawl, if that makes any sense. The *tout ensemble* was sweet and delicious, something like falling into a big butterscotch sundae, with her creamy skin and buttery hair, and smooth, soft voice. And she knew it.

You get more flies with honey, my mother used to say, and men would swarm like flies around this woman.

"See, some of my clients are so pleased to have met me—I'm just about the best thing in their lives. And, you know how it is when you have something you're proud of. You just want to tell the world about it, don't you, now?"

I said, "Of course." My voice would be cut in editing anyway.

"So they tell their friends, and their friends go, 'Why don't you introduce me to this wonderful woman? She sounds so—so sympathetic!' And my friend might say, 'Well, sure, I'll see about it.' Not that they would ever dare give out my number without asking me first. They are courteous to a *fault*. But if they tell me they vouch for the man, and he's a good—you know, a good person, not dangerous—then I'd tell them to give him my phone number."

"Where do you entertain your clients?"

"At home. At my home. I entertain them in my own home, just like anybody, anyone would. They call and they might say, 'Can I visit you tonight?' And I might say, 'I'm busy tonight, but how about tomorrow night around nine?' Like that."

"Do you have a p—'" "Pimp" was not going to be a word this woman liked. "Do you have a protector? Somebody who looks after your safety?"

"See, I have my own, wonderful boyfriend, and we have the most wonderful, mutually supportive relationship. We give each other space, but we're there for each other. He's a man who has come to terms with the masculine worldview of the nineties without losing his masculine appeal, and he comes around to my place a lot, or if I think there's a problem I call him to come over. And so he keeps things safe—like if I'm entertaining a friend I've never met before, then sometimes my boyfriend will wait around."

"You mean in the apartment?"

"Sure, honey. There's this little guest room where he can stay and nobody knows he's there, but if anything got, you know, out of line—well, then he's there, see?"

I thought they could edit that to a complete response by cutting the "Sure, honey," so I went on. "And he does what?"

"Well, he listens, and if he should hear any kind of fuss, like, if I was to call for help, except that never happens, my men friends are *so* gentlemanly, you wouldn't believe, but then he would come running."

This information ought to do something to the enthusiasm of the men who went to high-class prostitutes. The audience in the back room wouldn't appeal to me if I were one of those guys, that's for sure.

"How did you get into this line of work?"

Her face, usually languidly mobile, sank into an expressionless dullness. I felt like a heartless monster. But I let her think, or reminisce, or whatever she was doing, without interrupting. "Well, it's just one of those things," she said after half a minute. "You can't really expect somebody like me to cook hamburgers or wait tables. These are the best years of my life, beautywise. And I think I should make the most of it."

She was lying, or giving me a half-truth. "That brings up another question, Ms. Leleina. What will you do as time goes on?"

"Oh, I'm not going to be in this business forever. I'm very realistic. As a woman gets older, she loses her appeal. Men just go for the young woman, and that's the way it is. Always has been, always will be. No use crying over it. I'm already planning ahead. I'm just doing this long enough to get the money to open a model agency. That's something I'd be real good at, you know. If there's one thing in the world I understand, it's makeup, and how to walk, and...and whatever they need to know. Once I have the money for it, you watch me jump.''

"Can you describe your financial arrangements to me?''

"My men friends are the most generous people. You know how it is, if somebody is nice to you? You just want to do something nice in return? They have given me the most lovely jewelry. Why, last week, this man who is just the sweetest person, you wouldn't think he's said to be one of the toughest prosecutors in the whole city, bought me an emerald bracelet set in red gold? You know? It's things like that, the real appreciation, that makes life worthwhile.''

"What about money? Do your friends give you cash?''

She was not happy with that question. She recrossed her legs, a maneuver that did not have the effect on me it might have had on a male interviewer. I waited. She wanted to duck the question, but she must have given Ross her word that she'd be reasonably honest. I wondered just for a second what he had on her. Not my problem, though.

"Some of my good friends know how many expenses I have. There's rent, and you know how it is? When you're trying to keep up a pleasant environment for people to visit you where they can be comfortable and happy and relaxed? Why, then you have to have a nice place, don't you? It's an obligation, really. And some of my friends help me out with that.''

I wanted to ask her what she charged but wasn't quite sure whether she charged by the hour or the night, being as expensive as she apparently was. "Do your friends stay all night?"

"Sometimes they do."

That answer wouldn't work for the tape. Try again.

"Ms. Leleina, how does this work? Could you *describe* it for me? Does the gentleman caller tell you how long he wants to stay or what?" Now I was sounding like Tennessee Williams.

"My men friends either come by early, like six to eight, because after all, they have other obligations. They're important people and there are demands on their time, you see? Or otherwise they might come by later, like ten to twelve or so."

So she could accommodate two or more clients a night.

"Do you go out to dinner with them? Or parties?"

"Of course. Quite often."

"This next question, could you give me a longer answer, so we can use it better on the tape? Do you—ah—share your income with anybody? Your boyfriend, maybe?"

"Oh, sure, honey. Wait. A complete answer—um—I share my whole life and all with my boyfriend, and of course any money that comes in, well, he's just as welcome to as, as anything else."

"What proportion do you give him?"

"Proportion? You mean how much? Well, my boyfriend has expenses of his own, you know, and so I most generally pass on to him quite a bit of what I earn. That is, what gifts my friends give me. I suppose, maybe, three thousand out of every five. Right around in there. Sometimes a little more."

"You give him well over *half* of everything you take in?"

"Why, sure, honey, he's my boyfriend."

AFTERWARD, Felipe and I went to a diner for a sandwich.

"You seemed to find our interviewee easy to take," I said.

"You betcha. But then I spent most of last week with Channel Three's intrepid muckraker, Wilt Brandmeier. We were documenting spotty garbage pickup."

"Oh."

"Your lady smells better than last week's assignment."

"And looks better."

"Yup. You can't imagine some of the things people throw in the garbage. Dead cats and dogs, okay, you expect. A pet dies, where are they gonna bury it in the city? Under a fire hydrant?"

"Please!"

"But an ostrich?"

"You found an ostrich?"

"You betcha. You should've seen these *giant* claws sticking up outta the pile of black bags and old cartons and leaves. See, I figure somebody bought the ostrich as an investment, not a pet. Course you need at least two. Male and female. Breeding pair."

"I understand the concept of breeding pair."

"Because apparently there's a lot of ostrich ranches starting up in the south. Ostriches are valuable. They're gonna be used for meat and leather and feathers."

"But that's down south. What was your ostrich doing up here? What did the people who owned the garbage can say?"

"Said they'd never seen the thing before in their lives, and didn't want to see it now, neither. I believed 'em. I think somebody picked up a breeding pair at O'Hare, got as far as Chicago, and one of 'em died. Did you know a breeding pair is worth a couple of thousand dollars?"

"Didn't know that."

"And so what're you gonna do with a dead ostrich? They put it in the first big garbage can they saw."

"Public-spirited types, really," I said. "They could have dumped the poor thing in the street."

"Right." The waitress came, a young woman poking at her scalp with the tip of her pencil. "I'll have a hot dog," Felipe said.

Thinking about the dead cats and dogs, I said, "The broccoli omelet, please, with coffee."

Felipe said, "And a large Coke."

"You know," I mused, "that wouldn't have been a bad title of your garbage video essay."

"Which title?"

"'What Are You Gonna Do with a Dead Ostrich?'"

I WAS STILL WORRYING about how to shape the piece on Chicago prostitution. The channel had given me two weeks to work up the basic outline and tape the first interviews, which had seemed like a lot at the time. Newspaper editors, like Hal Briskman at *Chicago Today,* are likely to say, "This is Thursday. Have it on my desk by Monday morning." And they think they're doing you a favor by not saying, "This is Thursday. Have it on my desk by Friday at four."

Magazines generally allow a little longer—at least the glossies do, because their lead time is longer. But they usually want longer pieces, too, and the trade-off, moneywise, is not necessarily good.

When Zucrow at Channel Three gave me this assignment, last week Thursday, September third, he wasn't very specific. "Lotta hot air in the city council about prostitution right now," he said. "If we're gonna try using you, take a chance on you, this is a good subject. Right up your alley."

"Not literally, I assume?"

"What?"

"Up my alley? Prostitution? Very small joke. Never mind. Why do you say it's a good subject for me?"

"Oh, you've gotten into issues in the past where society is ambivalent about a question. The average citizen is against gambling, for instance, but in favor of the lottery. Against drugs, but we're the most medicated society on earth. Here's another one. We're against prostitution, no doubt about it. But if so, who's paying all those hookers?"

"Right. So exactly what kind of essay do you want?"

"Well, the aldermen have their shorts in an uproar because there's too many prostitutes on the streets. Find out if that's true."

"Sure. But how much is too much?"

"That's a point. Plus we want pathos in it. Or viciousness."

"Pathos or viciousness. Uh-huh."

"Now, the City Council wrangles are going to go on for maybe another three weeks. Then they want to adjourn for a long Thanksgiving vacation. In early October, mind you. They'll also want to show that they've made progress. So they may vote something by then."

"You're saying?"

"I want this thing to air in two weeks. Thursday, September seventeenth."

"And otherwise I can shape the essay the way I want?"

"More or less."

"Great!"

"As long as you don't screw up."

THIS WAS ONE of those things where the ball's in my court. Even if this had been a print article and not television, I would be going through some self-doubt. You may have written a hundred or maybe a thousand articles of one kind and another, but each time it's new. The problems are new. Particularly when it's a full essay on a subject, not just a quick reporting job of facts or events. And every time, it's intimidating. Will I come up with a lead that makes people want to read it? Will the subject be interesting? Can I be as accurate as I want to be in the amount of time I have to do the research? As of today, I had nine days left.

About the only reassurance you have at the beginning of a major project is that you've done them before and it worked out. You were not fired. You did not make a fool of yourself.

But Zucrow was putting a lot of pressure on me, and the medium was new to me. The time frame seemed enough, but without much slack, and I didn't know how much would be consumed by editing. The only thing to do was to jump in.

You have to start somewhere. Suppose an editor said, "There's a marbles Olympics in town. I want an article on marbles."

You'd say, "The game?"

"No, marbles themselves."

So you go to a collector and he rolls a thousand marbles onto the floor for you to see. Okay, you've got more marbles than you know what to do with. Big marbles, tiny marbles, some precious stone, some brass, some steel, maybe jade and topaz—you get the picture. You can't just look at this chaos and "write a story." What do you do? You can't talk about every marble and you can't even cover all the categories that might describe all the marbles, either; you have to choose. You think—maybe I can organize this by color, like the rainbow, make a rainbow of marbles—violet, indigo, blue, green, yellow, orange, and red. Or maybe not. Doesn't go anywhere. Maybe you can organize by size. Or maybe not. Not interesting. Doesn't set the imagination racing. Maybe the different values of marbles would be more interesting. The inexpensive kind you can buy by the dozens in a string bag. The more expensive ones of metal and stone. The very precious one-of-a-kind marbles with cloisonné surfaces or gold tracing.

Maybe there's a history of marbles—how they developed, how the games of marbles are played. Maybe there were famous historical persons who collected marbles.

Or maybe the best thing would be just to collect all the purple ones, all the various shades of purple, and show how much range some items that are basically similar can have.

But before you start, you have to get down on the floor and look at those marbles. You don't have to look at every one of the thousand in detail, but you have to sit among them, and move them around, play with them, and see what you've got.

And if you ask me, you're a lot better off if you don't get down there with too many preconceptions. Otherwise, you may impose yourself and your ideas on the material. Or you may write an article that's suggested by other articles you've read on the same subject and therefore has no freshness.

So, okay. I didn't know much from personal observation about prostitution, and at the same time I had read too much. I had to shake my head clear of all that and look at the subject with new eyes.

What I use at these times is total immersion. Random total immersion, you might call it. I get into the subject wherever and however I can. It doesn't so much matter where you start, as long as you keep rooting around.

In this case, one obvious way to go would be interviews in depth with one or two hookers. How they got into the life, that kind of thing. I wanted to do that with Sandra. Another possibility was to focus on the actual, day-to-day operation of, say, an escort service. How are the women paid? Where does the money go? How do they recruit? Another was to focus on what happens to the hookers in the long run. How many ever get out of the game? How many get into another line of work or retire? How many even survive to get old? Find some sick, aging women. A tearjerker. Zucrow's preference, probably.

I'd have to make a decision on which way to go very soon. But for now, I was still exploring.

One of the first sources I turned to was the Chicago Yellow Pages. The letting-your-fingers-do-the-walking kind of research is really a relief at times. Problems with parking in Chicago suck out your energy after a while. Chicago weather can get wearing, too—leave the apartment in the morning in the sunshine and come home in a sleet storm. Footwork is hard work.

I went home in the late afternoon, after the interview with Ms. Leleina. I curled up on my secondhand but perfectly adequate sofa. Long John Silver swooped down and sat on my shoulder. He likes it when I sit and read. Not as much as he likes being played with, having his Nerf ball rolled away so he can attack it. But he does enjoy a quiet evening at home reading books. This probably dates back to his years with the English professor.

LJ can't read, but he cocks his head and looks at each page. That is, I'm pretty sure he can't read. Positive. Birds don't read, not even talking birds. Not even talking birds who are very, very smart.

Naturally, I checked "prostitutes" in the Yellow Pages and found no listing. Didn't expect any. But it's important not to overlook the obvious. Next I looked for "escort services." There wasn't any such listing. There may be in other parts of the country, but not in Chicago.

Okay, what next? Exotic dancers? No. Dancers? No. Dating services? Aha. Here was something.

Lots of dating services. You could call for a "lady" who would enhance your business or social function. Several agencies called themselves "escort services" in their descriptions, even if there was no such general listing. One was titled "Amore. Male escorts." Say, I could research that directly—no, hold it, Marsala. That's not what I was supposed to be doing in this essay. Women only. Some agencies listed were clearly legit or reasonably legit matchmaking services. Some clearly weren't. I guessed that the code words were "adult," "all services available," and possibly "fantasy" and "exotic."

Altogether, though, there weren't so very many that were obvious fronts for prostitution. Maybe twelve to fifteen.

What other listings might they be hiding under? Entertainment? Entertainers?

Ah, yes. Here, among the magicians for kid's parties, hire-a-disc-jockeys, puppeteers, orchestra, comics, handwriting analysts, and even Rent A Nerd, were many of the same listings from the dating services pages. And a few extras. Exotic dancers, who might be legit. Strippers. Maybe they were legit, too. Who knows?

One advertised a pregnant stripper. How amusing can that be? And how do they keep getting performers?

Rent A Honey? Great. Very classy. "Sophisticated companions" seemed like another hooker code word for the experienced devotee.

The ones I was most suspicious of were the listings without addresses or any descriptive remarks at all. Things like ExStacy with nothing but dots... followed by a phone number. Or Rita's Talent Agency dot-dot-dot... and a phone number.

I tried looking up everything else that came to mind. Massage? Well, a few that set the mind wondering, but nothing clearly useful. Stress management? No. Physical therapists? Not really.

Finally, I made a list of a dozen names and addresses, including Beau Monde ("Sophisticated Companions"), that seemed obviously to be escort services with a hookerish leaning. And I surmised they had to be reasonably obvious if they were going to be successful, because if a man was looking in the Yellow Pages and couldn't find them, how were they going to get customers and make money?

Telephoning them might tell me something. Taking a look at their offices, if they really had offices and not just a mail drop, might be informative, too.

As I was going through the Yellow Pages listings, I found myself wincing or snickering at some of the entries. Rent A Dream. Really! Then I caught myself at it.

My behavior was no better than that of all the high
school boys I had known years back with their own
snickering and whore jokes. The women who had become prostitutes were people, after all, and people in
pretty desperate circumstances for one reason or another.

Going into this project, I'd thought a lot about my
attitude toward the subject. As long as I kept that bar-
ricade between the hookers and me, as long as I thought
of them as "them" and of myself as a different species,
this investigation wasn't going to work, or at least
wouldn't really take off. For one thing, I just wouldn't
have the rapport with the women that was needed to get
them talking and develop an honest interview. Also, I
wouldn't be able to understand what they did, why they
did it, how they lived, and how they managed to put up
with their lives.

I was going to have to listen, not just hear. However
incomprehensible a hooker's life seemed to me now, I
was going to have to understand.

SIX

By the time I exhausted the information in the Yellow Pages and made a list of the places I wanted to visit, it was six o'clock. This was the first afternoon in a long time that I hadn't spent running around the city, either on foot or in the old Bronco.

Long John Silver was still sitting on my shoulder. How Old World and piratical we must have looked, if not for the soft light of the word processor monitor glowing happily in the kitchen.

My apartment is extremely small. Because I am living in tight quarters, my work space is the kitchen table. This means my dining space is the sofa.

I got up without dislodging LJS, indolent bird that he is, and padded out to the kitchen in stocking feet. Six P.M., and what could I cook?

"Well, LJ, we have a jar of peanut butter in the refrigerator, several ribs of celery here in the veggie drawer—hmm, a jar of chutney, some sliced Swiss cheese. Gee, these cheese slices are about as stiff as roofing shingles."

"Gaaaaak!" said LJ. He was right, too.

"Let's check our cupboards. Rice. Brown and white rice both. My goodness, we're well provided for. A can of refried beans. What about down here?"

In the lower cupboard where I keep onions and garlic and potatoes, there were only onions. But that was okay. "Zowie! This will be a feast."

LJ swooped to the floor and grabbed an onion skin. He gobbled it down, his big wrinkled eyes blinking in delight.

"Easy to please you!" I said, speaking an untruth.

I boiled some rice, heated the refried beans, chopped onions over the whole business, and half an hour later was sitting on my sofa, thrilled and delighted to be having a quiet evening at home. LJ played with his Nerf ball and occasionally flapped over to me. I fed him little pieces of celery.

Nothing to nag me. Nothing to bother me. Nobody to cater to. What bliss!

I pulled over a pad of paper and tried out a possible introduction to the television essay. How about something like:

"Prostitution has been called the oldest profession. People less enthusiastic call it the second-oldest profession. It probably isn't either one. In fact, it probably isn't even close. In the context of early man, toolmaker or even weapon maker was probably the oldest profession. Mercenary soldiers came in early on. For millennia the most desirable women were simply taken by force by the strongest males.

"But prostitution is certainly an old profession. Old but not any more respectable because of its age. Prostitutes work the streets and hotels and homes of Chicago. This isn't news to anybody. But there are certain differences in Chicago today—"

Yes, but what differences? Drugs? Well, before drugs it was drink. Is anything really new? What exactly did I want to say? How in the world was I going to organize this damn thing?

Writing is thinking written down, and if your head isn't clear about the subject, the printed page won't be clear, either.

I settled back and folded my legs up on the sofa. I munched a little more of the beans and rice. It was so good to have a little time for peaceful reflection, without being hassled.

"This is the life, huh, Long John?"

"Awwwk!" LJ said. "Life makes strange bedfellows!"

"LJ, you're pretty convincing, but you just hear a word I say and then repeat it with some other things you've heard before."

"Awk!"

"For instance, who wrote 'Life makes strange bedfellows'?"

"Awwk!"

"Well, neither do I, but I know how to look it up."

I slouched over to the bookcase. I buy up all the reference works I can find at used-book stores and events like the giant Brandeis Used-Book Sale on the north shore. A reference book is far less expensive than a trip to a specialty library—particularly if you have to park your car in a lot.

I curled up again on the sofa and rummaged in Mencken's *New Dictionary of Quotations.* Which took a while. Obviously everyone in the world had said something about what life was really like. Life was like a fever. Life was like a hill, you go up one side and down the other. Life was dreary. Life was shining. Was it Neil Simon who said, "Life isn't everything"?

"Aha! See?" I held the book out to LJ. "Bulwer-Lytton said life makes strange bedfellows! You didn't know that."

"Awwk," he said, on a softer note. He sat on my lap and looked sideways at me out of one big, wrinkled eye. His eyes seemed to me to contain the ancient primitive wisdom of reptiles, on earth millennia before man. I ran my hand down his back and he blinked. One piece of celery was left on the plate, and I fed it to him.

Peace and quiet.

The door buzzer buzzed.

I dragged myself out of the sofa. If this was Mike, come to make new promises to break, he was going to hear a few choice words.

Being a city dweller, when I leaned over to look down the stairwell at the small window in the front door and saw nobody, I locked my door and yelled, "Who's there?"

"Andy."

"I don't know any Andy."

"Andy. Please."

I still couldn't see anybody through the glass panel. Well, it was a woman's voice, and it couldn't hurt to go down and look closer.

"I'm coming."

The glass panel was high in the door, on the theory that burglars couldn't reach the inside knob even if they broke the glass. This was probably true, as long as the burglar didn't bring a step stool. Usually, if the visitor was tall enough and was standing in the right place, I could see down through it from my third-floor hall. But from the vestibule here it was harder. I was too short. I had to jump up to look through the glass.

Which I did. And couldn't see. It was too late at night—even though it wasn't past seven—for this kind of thing. "Hey! Look up!" I said to whoever it was. I jumped again.

A pale face stared up at me in the split second I was airborne.

"Sandra!"

SHE SAT ON THE SOFA, drinking hot tea with lots of sugar. The tea hurt her mouth, because her mouth was bruised and her upper lip swollen to twice its normal thickness. It didn't seem to be cut, but she yelped when the heat touched it.

"Drink the tea anyway," I said. "You need sugar when you've been hurt."

She complied meekly. She was in her waif mode. The only hint of a glamorous woman was the short green skirt she wore and a blue-green shimmery blouse. The blouse was ripped on the right shoulder, and under the rip were bright-red splotches that looked like finger-marks. Her left ear was red and swelling, and the skin above it on the temple showed a bluish bump about the size of half an egg. Her makeup was smeared.

I got some ice from the refrigerator and put it into a washcloth.

"Hold this on your head. Try to get it on the ear and just above it—that's right—right there."

During the procedure, LJ was hopping around, flit-ting from the arm of the sofa to the curtain rod to the top of the television set to the Nerf ball. It said a lot about Sandra's stunned passivity that she saw him hop-ping around and yet never asked what he was or why I had him. Not even when he said, "Call me Ishmael."

While she held the ice to her ear, I rummaged in the kitchen, eventually coming up with some crackers. On these I spread what was left of the jar of peanut butter and took them in to Sandra.

"Thanks."

"What happened?"

"Well, my boyfriend kind of slapped me around."

"Let's start with the assumption that I am not an idiot, or we won't get anyplace. Nobody slapped you around. Somebody punched you in the face. Then somebody took hold of your right shoulder and shoved you into a wall. Hard."

She stared at me, her eyes big. After a few seconds, she said, "Well, yeah."

"Who?"

"My boyfr—my father."

"Why?"

"Well, because he caught up with me, see. That's why I came here. He just found out where I live. But he'd never think of looking here."

"What exactly—watch it! He'll eat all the peanut butter!"

I waved LJ away from her snack. She needed it more than he did. "What exactly," I repeated, "do you want me to do?"

"I'd like to stay here overnight." She said it without inflection, as if she had no idea which way I would go. As if she had no idea where she'd be an hour from now.

Not that I knew, either. "Why here?"

"I had your card—"

"No, I know how you found me. I mean, why?"

"You seemed understanding. I think you're a kind person."

"Sandra, listen. Don't you really mean that it seemed to you that I wanted something? An interview. And you might be able to barter what I wanted for what you wanted?"

"Barter?"

"Make a deal?"

"Well, we could do that, couldn't we?"

Wasn't this what I had been looking for? The story in depth? The answer to what made Sandra tick?

I was about to try to be simultaneously firm and accommodating, but the door buzzed again. Now what?

I looked down the stairwell. This person was tall enough for me to see and he was standing where I could see him. John. I buzzed the door.

Now we had a small party.

"This is John Banks, Sandra. Sandra Lupica, John."

Sandra said, "Hi."

John said, "How do you do?" John tends to be formal on first meeting anybody. Partly this is a result of being brought up by a mother who couldn't distinguish between manners and courtesy, but partly he believes that people feel more respected by a slightly formal approach first. He's capable of loosening up later.

This time he didn't. He had a pastry box under his arm. John is aware that flowers and jewelry and such are not nearly as effective an approach to my heart as chocolate. Now he held the box close to his chest. He had expected me to be alone, sure, but that wasn't all of it. I had mentioned Sandra to him and he knew immediately who this was and what she was.

It would have been cowardly to put off explaining and dishonest to try to fool him. Naturally, I considered both options. Rejected them on the grounds that I might be found out. It's good to have these clear values.

"John, Sandra is staying here tonight. But why don't we sit down and I'll make some coffee?"

Sandra shuffled her feet. John said nothing.

"Or I can make tea. Maybe I have some ginger ale."

"Uh, tea, please," John said. Then I watched realization go through his mind, just as if the thoughts were visible. He realized that if I were in the kitchen boiling water, he would be in the living room, the tiny living room, trying to make conversation with a prostitute.

"Ginger ale," he said.

Sandra said, "Fine with me."

I took a little longer pouring the ginger ale than absolutely necessary. My ear was aimed toward the living room. Since the distance was all of about twelve feet, it wasn't difficult to hear.

"Uh—did you drop by just now?" John said.

Sandra, not surprisingly, was more adept at getting males into conversation than John was at chatting without referring to what she did for a living. Or the reason for the condition of her face (which would have been rude to ask about).

Sandra said, "Yes. So, you're a friend of Cat's?"

"Yes. Known her a long time."

"What's your work, John?"

"I'm a stockbroker."

"Oh, that's wonderful. I know several stockbrokers."

Silence. John trying hard, I suppose, not to ask her *how* she knows them.

"It must be very difficult work, being a stockbroker. People constantly calling to complain when some stock goes down. And never giving you any credit when they go up."

She certainly *had* met stockbrokers.

"Absolutely! Happens all the time. When stocks go up, the customer always thinks he was smart to agree to buy it. And when it goes down, he thinks you talked him into it against his will." John suddenly realized he'd been seduced, verbally speaking. "Um—sometimes," he added lamely. "Some clients are perfectly reasonable people, of course."

"Yes, I suppose that's true," Sandra said, musingly.

I took pity on him. "Here's the ginger ale, group! One for you, one for you, and one for me." This reminded me that there was another person in the room, or at least another creature. Where was LJ? He loved John, and ordinarily swooped down and talked with him, or pretended to talk.

But LJ was sitting on the curtain rod. His head was swiveling back and forth, trying to make out the social situation. Very cautious bird.

John, whose ears were bright pink, had drained his ginger ale in one long gulp. "Well, I'll have to be going."

I said, "So soon?"

Sandra said, "So soon?"

"I'm afraid so. Cat—just a word with you?"

"Sure."

He stepped outside the door, into the hall, and I followed.

"Cat, you know I never give you advice."

"Well, you used to. But you've been doing better at holding back."

"I think I have a responsibility to warn you about this. This is not a good idea, having that woman in your house."

"I appreciate your concern. Why are we out here whispering in the hall?"

"It would be rude to hurt her feelings."

"You don't want to be rude to her, but you want me to turn her out in the night?"

"Cat, she's a hooker!"

"I know that."

"She's probably on some kind of drugs."

"Coke, I think."

"Jeez!"

"But she seems to have got off it. Temporarily, anyhow. She said she was trying. Anyway, you notice she's not sniffling."

"Cat! I don't believe you'd do this! The woman may steal you blind."

"Steal what? A lifetime collection of Levi's? A used sofa? Maybe my collection of art? Hell, even my poster of the Wicked Witch from *Snow White* is a reproduction."

"Suppose she steals your word processor?"

"Oh. Well, that *would* be serious." Very serious. However, it was used, and insured, and also pretty clumsy to carry around. "I'll back up all the data before I go to bed tonight, just in case."

"You're not taking this seriously. You don't have any idea what she's into. Whoever hit her may come around tonight looking to get her and get even with whoever's helping her."

"Isn't that more reason to give her a safe place to stay? Seriously, John. You're asking me to turn an injured woman out on the streets at night when there's obviously somebody out there who doesn't like her."

"I will spare you the remark that she's been on the streets before."

"No, you didn't spare me!" I was getting angry. "You just said it, and it's a cheap shot, too!"

"There are places that will take in people like her."

"Where?"

"I don't know, but I can find out."

"Tonight?"

"Well. Maybe."

"They'll take battered women, sure. But battered hookers?"

"Uh. I don't know."

"And will they be pleasant? And will they really be safe? Because this place, however small and inelegant it is, is pretty safe. Locks on the windows—"

"As a result of your last catastrophe."

"Yes, but I have them now. Locks downstairs. Locks on this door."

"You don't know anything about her!"

"I know quite a lot about her! Unfortunately, it's all bad!"

"Take her someplace, Cat! This is insane!"

"She's staying here! And that's all there is to it!"

He stopped talking and closed his eyes. When he opened them again, his voice was lower and sadder.

"You are just so damn stubborn. I can't deal with this. Sane, ordinary, intelligent people, no matter how kindly, do not take hookers into their homes. She's lived her life without your help up to now."

"You're being heartless."

"Maybe. Maybe to her. Not to you. But you don't see it that way."

I didn't say anything. This was my home and my decision and I was still angry. Frightened of losing John, but angry at the same time. Better if I didn't say anything.

My refusal to speak was the final straw. "Here!" he said, pushing the bakery box, which he was still carrying, toward me. "Sacher torte slices. I hope the two of you enjoy them!"

THE HELL OF IT WAS, I had the nagging feeling that John was right. This was a stupid act. But I just could not manage to put her out on the street. Yes, she'd been out on the street before in her life. But not shoved out by me.

When I got back inside after watching sadly as John stomped away and slammed the front door, she was sitting curled up on the sofa. LJ was still on the curtain rod watching her. I put the pastry box on the television set and sat facing her on the only other chair in the room.

"I'm sorry about this," she said in a small voice.

"Wait a minute." I didn't want to be cruel. But I also was not a total moron and the little-girl-lost approach didn't appeal to me as much as it might have to a man.

"Sandra, you can stay here for a while. A *short* while. We're going to try to figure out what to do for you. But I can't keep you for long. I'm...too much of a loner for that. Plus it wouldn't help you in the long run."

"Okay. Okay. I understand."

"Now, I'll make up a bed for you on the sofa." Fortunately, even though my sofa had been bought used and cheap, it was big. "In the morning, we'll talk about what you want to do."

"Okay."

"Here's a towel and a glass. The bathroom's in there. Put your towel on the towel rack to the left of the bowl. Take a shower if you want. No, maybe you'd be better off not getting hot water on the bruises right now. Anyway, I'll have this made up by the time you get done."

Half an hour later, I was lying in my bed trying to go to sleep. My bedroom door was closed. LJ was in here with me, in his cage. I wondered whether Sandra was sleeping. Would she steal everything and leave in the night? Or on the other hand, would she be impossible to get rid of?

Long John Silver produced a little pigeonlike *cooooo*, which he sometimes does when he's falling asleep. Then it hit me. Maybe LJ was prescient. Earlier this evening, had he known what was coming when he said life makes strange bedfellows?

SEVEN

WHEN I WOKE UP the next morning, I thought about the person who wakes up in bed with a stranger. Fortunately, this is a mistake I've either been lucky enough or smart enough to avoid, but the knowledge that Sandra was out there in the living room was damn close. It had all the elements:

What have I done?

And how am I going to get rid of her?

It was very late for me to be getting up—past ten A.M. I opened LJ's cage and crept out of my room. Sure enough, there was Sandra, asleep on the sofa. She had not stolen everything portable and left. Now what? There was very little food in the place. Okay, I'd let her sleep and go out and get some edibles.

One advantage of living in this neighborhood, which is an odd mix of apartments, warehouses, offices, fruit stands, art galleries, cheap restaurants, delis, and trendy food stores, is that you can find almost anything within four or five blocks at almost any time. It was Thursday, September tenth, and I was uneasily aware that I had seven days to air date. Today I'd have to get moving.

Back in ten minutes with still-warm bagels, cream cheese, a quarter pound of butter, a dozen eggs, a coffee cake, and a quart of milk, I found Sandra sitting up rubbing her eyes. She looked like a little girl. Well, after all, she was only nineteen, so it wasn't so amazing she looked young.

For just a couple of seconds I wondered about how young she would look ten years from now. Ten years from now she would be only twenty-nine, younger than I was today, but her life-style wasn't going to treat her well. If she went on with her life-style.

Hold it right there, Marsala. You're thinking of saving her from herself and putting her feet on the path toward clean productive living, aren't you? Get real.

Sandra must have caught a whiff of the just-baked bagels. She said, "Oh, that smells great!"

"Come on in." I headed into the kitchen. LJ flapped along after me.

Usually, coming down from coke, if that was what she was doing, ruins a person's appetite. Not hers, apparently. She was droopy, though, which was consistent, and she sniffled now and then. My guess was that she inhaled whatever she used, probably cocaine, rather than injecting it, and probably coke itself, not the crack form. She was, as the cops and dopers put it, a tootin' head.

She had not brought any clothes with her, so she wore the blue-green shimmering shirt that she had arrived in, the one with the torn sleeve. It did not look anywhere near as glamorous in the morning light. Not just because of the rip. The fabric, even the color, looked tawdry. She, however, was looking much better in this third persona—pretty, rested, and young.

I toasted two bagel halves, handed her one, and put two more in the toaster. By the time I turned around she had spread an inch of cream cheese on top of hers.

"Jeez! I wish I could eat like that and not gain weight!" I said.

"I'm lucky, I guess. I've never gained weight all that easily."

Wasn't this cozy?

We munched bagels in companionable silence, but a memory was teasing the back left corner of my mind. When I was in grade school I had had a best friend named Molly. Molly and I did everything together. We went through that stage where nine-year-old girls desperately wish they owned horses. We galloped around the neighborhood, pretending we were riding horses. For some reason this involved loping along in a kind of hop, with the right foot always forward and the left foot always back.

We dressed Barbie dolls. When we got into junior high school we spent endless hours in front of the mirror in my bedroom with combs, trying French twists, goofy bouffant things, severe buns, ponytails, and braids.

In early high school we still did hair, but by then Molly's mother had bought her a hot comb and we got more ambitious. And we started doing our hair before dates.

And then, in tenth grade, Molly got pregnant.

It was like the sun had burned out. Suddenly Molly didn't come to school anymore. Her father, always a stern man, was said to be so furious her mother kept them apart. I called Molly a couple of times, but she wouldn't talk much.

Then I stopped calling. She never came back to school. People whispered about her, and some said the baby had been given up for adoption. Molly was working as a waitress in a diner. There was some snickering on the part of several boys that waitressing wasn't all she was working at.

I had scarcely thought of her in years. And the reason was that deep down I felt guilty. I had behaved badly toward Molly. I should have gone on calling until she wanted to talk. Until she realized I meant it and wasn't just calling out of some temporary sense of obligation.

Looking back, I suppose I wanted to distance myself from her, which wasn't very nice, either. Molly had become an outcast, and beyond that, teenage girls like me, who weren't "sexually active," were at an age to be confused and embarrassed about the whole thing.

It was not nice of me to leave her alone to whatever future she might have.

Molly had been red haired and pale skinned and looked quite a lot like Sandra. Not exactly. Molly's hair was a more carroty red, and her skin was a lighter, freckly white. But they were similar enough.

They were not the same person, and it was not necessary to get sucked into Sandra's problems, just because she reminded me of Molly. Even though she may have reminded me of Molly from the first, and I just hadn't realized it until now.

It was important to keep a clear notion of who and what Sandra was.

Sometime back then, too, in high school, I had read a story in which the narrator asked whether future events cast dark shadows before them. Would we have a feeling of impending disaster before it happened? If so, he said, shouldn't we feel the chill breath each year when the calendar brings around the day on which we will die?

I wondered later if I had a sense that Sandra's future was dark.

Sandra asked if she could use my bubble bath. I said she could. A bath would get her out of my way for a while, while I finished writing up my notes from yesterday and the evening before with Ross. Thank goodness for word processors. I could type everything in as I'd heard it, a line for each item, and when it came time to do the final piece, just pull the items whole and plug them in. Then smooth and fix—

Sandra had entered the bathroom a little before noon. I glanced at the clock. It was after one, and she was still in there, singing snatches of popular music, now and then splashing and running more water. Gusts of lilac bubble-bath perfume wafted out under the door. Gee, she'd look like a prune when she got out.

But she didn't look like a prune. She looked very pretty, bruises notwithstanding, when she emerged. In *my* bathrobe.

I was about to draw breath and ask her some hard questions when she said, "Look. I know I just dropped in on you, here."

" Well—"

"But I'm not a freeloader. I really intend to pay my way. I'll do the interview."

"Well, okay. That's great." Why wasn't I more excited? There was a sound of reserve in her voice, that's why. She must have some serious reason to want to stay here, but at the same time, I was getting vibes that during the interview she might not speak from the heart.

"Do you mean you'll do the interview with me today?"

"If that's what you want."

"Because I can call my cameraman, if you really mean it." Reporters learn to strike while the iron is hot; more than one interviewee upon reflection has thought better of it and backed out.

I went to the phone and called Felipe. Yes, he could come over immediately. In fact, he understood the problem and said he'd take a taxi. "They'll pay for that kind of thing," he said. I gave him the address.

I asked, "Will my place be okay?"

"What do you mean?"

"To film. Tape. I don't live in the Ambassador Towers."

"Oh, listen, that's even better. We need as many backgrounds as possible. Sometimes, when we have to interview people out of town at hotels and stuff, you know—"

"Yes?"

"We rent two or three different rooms and carry around a lot of changes of paintings and drapes and stuff, just so it'll look different."

"Oh." I felt like an idiot. There was so little I knew about this business. Pay attention, Marsala! Learn!

"He'll be here in forty-five minutes or so," I said to Sandra.

He was at the door in half an hour.

"SO—LET ME EXPLAIN how this works," I said, and gave her the pep talk about full-sentence answers. She caught on immediately. She was bright, which made the whole thing even sadder. And I was deeply aware that she was granting this interview as a kind of quid pro quo. She didn't want to do it, but she was paying me for letting her stay here. I was buying her, too, wasn't I, just as other people did. I felt guilty.

Guilty enough not to do the interview? Nope.

"Have you decided whether you want the interview digitalized? So you won't be recognized?"

"No." She smiled at last. "Maybe with these bruises I won't be recognized anyhow."

"I have to be honest. They don't show much under the makeup. I'd know you. Close friends would *surely* know you."

"Well, let's see how I feel later. Okay?"

"Fine with me."

Felipe said, "We're ready to roll."

I planned to take her through the easier material first and slide on up to hard questions later, like how she got into this line of work.

"Let's discuss the mechanics of an escort service. How do customers hear about the service?"

"Most of the men hear about our service from other men. They hear them talking about the name. But still, a lot of our customers are from out of town and don't know. Sometimes they ask a taxi driver or a hotel concierge. Lots of times, they just look in the phone book."

"All right. They call the phone number. What happens next?"

"When they call, they get our office manager, who finds out what it is they want. I mean, some men are in town and going to a dinner or whatever, and they want to take a woman along. It makes them look—uh—successful. So they want a girl who can talk well. Or gay men might want to look straight. Or local men who don't have woman in their lives might want an escort for a special occasion. Like a company dinner. Or a major New Year's Eve party. Like that."

It was astonishing how well she had followed my instructions about using full sentences. This was one swift person. I hated to press her. However, even in my business, business is business.

"But not all these men are calling just for a pretty woman to take to a party."

"No." A short answer. She corrected herself with no prompting: "A lot of the men who call just want sex."

"Does the woman who answers the phone take orders for sex specifically?"

"The woman who answers the phone is very careful not ever to say that she's taking an order for sex. She never says anything like 'It'll cost three hundred for this or five hundred for that.' She says things like 'Our young women can spend an hour at your function for three hundred.' So if anybody is listening in, there's never any word at all about taking money for sex."

"All right. How does the office manager decide which woman to send where?"

"A lot of the men who call like a certain type of woman. And our office manager always asks whether they prefer a blonde or brunette or what. It's a funny thing, but the ones who want you to go out to some party or dinner with them first usually tell right away what height of woman they want. I mean, they'll say something like 'I want a pretty girl, but not over five feet six.' They're real worried about getting somebody taller than they are. I get a lot of those assignments, because I'm kind of short." She smiled again, very briefly.

"Also," she said, "I get a lot of those assignments where they say, 'I want somebody who can *talk*.' That means we're going out with friends or people from the company or whatever first, and they don't want somebody who sounds like an idiot."

This small source of pride seemed to relax her.

"Sandra, this suggests that the escort service basically lets you explain what you will do for what money. So that it won't go on their phone line. Right?"

"Um. We explain to the customer what services he can buy."

She was giving me a complete-sentence answer but backing away from the nitty-gritty. Felipe noticed it, too, and gave me a glance. In fact, while Sandra had been answering all my questions with apparent honesty, I was getting the feeling that it was coming over as pretty dry stuff. She was factual, but there wasn't any emotion in it and not much impression of Sandra's character.

What was I going to do? I was a novice at this.

"Sandra, how do the men pay for the service?"

"Cash or credit cards. Sorry. Most of the customers pay for the service with cash or credit cards. The out-of-town customers almost all pay with credit cards. I think they want to charge it on their expense accounts, if they can."

"How is it itemized?"

"I write in 'entertainment' on the item line."

"You mean you carry a thing to take an impression of their credit cards?"

"I take an impression of their credit cards. My stamp doesn't have the name of the escort service. The men wouldn't want their wives to catch on. It says SJR Systems. And I give them the customer copy, just like a restaurant or whatever."

I glanced at Felipe again. Out of Sandra's view behind the camera—she was looking at her left knee, anyhow—he raised his eyebrows. It was pretty obvious what he meant.

"No matter what—um—kind of things they want?"

"When a customer asks for a, sort of, some special service, we just quote a higher price—and we, you know, get the account charged and have him sign the slip before—"

The phone rang. Felipe said, "We'll have to redo that." He didn't sound entirely distressed at the interruption.

"Okay. Let me get the phone."

It was Ross. "We're supposed to be meeting today, aren't we?"

"Yes, I thought so."

"Well, how about we come by your place about—mmm, about four o'clock? You're only a couple blocks from the Eighteenth, and we're gonna be on our way south anyhow."

"Uh—" I was thinking about the complications of having a cop stop by with Sandra here. He could spook her. Also, "we" who? But what could go wrong? Maybe I could meet them downstairs when they rang the bell. "Okay. Sounds fine."

When I turned back toward the sofa, I had decided to give Sandra a short break and hope that it would loosen her up. "Felipe, how about if I toast some bagels? Is that okay?"

"You betcha."

"And maybe some tea?"

Felipe clicked off his supplementary lights. He said, "You got coffee?"

"Sure."

"Let me make it. You Anglo people don't make coffee strong enough. And I'll toast the bagels while I'm doing it."

I was going to snap back that *my* coffee was strong enough, but something in his face said, Marsala shut up. He wanted me to get Sandra warmed up. Sure.

"Sandra, does it make you nervous, having the camera on?"

"No, I don't think so. How do I look?"

"Fine. Actually, the bruises don't show in the lights. I suppose this is hard to talk about."

"Sort of."

Well, she certainly wasn't helping me much. It seemed possible she was coming down from a cocaine high, or more likely just felt the dullness that she might if she wanted some. I moved over to sit next to her.

"Are you all right?"

"Pretty much."

What could I do? Take her hand? Tell her we cared? She'd probably had more than enough people tell her they cared, then pay her and disappear.

"Braak!" said LJ. "Call me Ishmael!"

"Good thing you didn't do that while the camera was running," I said to him.

Sandra stared at LJ. LJ sat on the curtain rod, turning his head from side to side.

Suddenly LJ took off, like a paper airplane thrown by a child. He swooped across the living room and landed on Sandra's shoulder. I jumped up to grab him, knowing how his claws could prick the skin if he gripped too hard.

Sandra was staring at him, her eyes wide.

"Pretty bird! Pretty bird!" LJ said, going back to some childhood or chickhood memory. And he rubbed his beak on her ear. This was exactly what he usually did with John.

"Pretty! Pretty! Pretty!" LJ cooed.

Sandra burst into tears.

I jumped up. "Bad parrot!" I said. "Bad bird!"

But Sandra was there to block me. "He's not bad!"

"Is he hurting your shoulder?"

"No!"

"Then what—"

Sandra reached up and very tentatively ran her hand down LJ's back. He rubbed his beak on her ear again, saying, "Pretty, pretty, pretty, pretty."

"He loves me," Sandra said, tears still pooling under her eyes and spilling over her cheeks. She touched his horny, reptilian toes with her index finger. "He loves me. Just as if I was somebody."

Out of the corner of my eye, I saw Felipe come out of the kitchen door carrying a plate of bagels, then stop and back into the kitchen. He was out of Sandra's sight because she was facing partly toward me, while I was facing her.

"He loves me. No matter what."

Gingerly, I sat back down. "I'm sure he does. And he's quite fussy about who he likes, too."

"I haven't been telling you the truth. It was my boyfriend who hit me. Not my father. But my father would if he could." She was still crying, gulping, occasionally swiping away tears. Between the red eyes, the bruises, and the now-puffy lips, she looked a mess.

"So it's your boyfriend you want to get away from."

"No, it's both of them. My father's in town. He was looking for me. But when he hits me, he doesn't hit me in the face. He—he—"

"What?"

"He hits me in the stomach. Or he spanks me."

"At your age? He spanks you?"

"Yes."

She started to rub her eyes furiously. I said, "Wait! Let me get you a wet cloth."

I went into the kitchen and ran cold water on a clean towel. Felipe raised his eyebrows at me. He had the water for the coffee boiling and was about to pour it over the grounds in the Chemex. Without speaking—after all, we were ten feet, tops, from Sandra's back—I held my thumb and index finger about an inch apart, signifying, I hoped, that he should wait just a little longer before coming into the living room.

"Here. This is cool water. Pat, don't rub."

She took the towel and pressed it all over her face. Then, like the child she really was, she rubbed her face hard with it anyway.

"Do I look awful?"

"Kind of. Here." I took the towel and brushed the hair back from her face. I patted her wet eyes, and brushed at her eyebrows a little with the towel, upward, since she had left them draggled down. "Got a comb?"

She handed me a pocket comb, and while I combed her hair, Felipe walked in saying, "Coffee, anybody?"

Half a bagel and some coffee later, she said, "I'll talk to the camera some more. I really would like to, I think."

I had misgivings about taping her while she was in this condition. It was a case of using what might be a passing mood—using her vulnerability for the benefit of my story. These misgivings made me pause easily four or five seconds.

She could review the tape later, if she wanted to, and if she absolutely insisted, we could take out parts that were too sensitive.

"I don't think I want that parrot on her shoulder in the shot," Felipe said.

"Here. Let me get him—"

Sandra said, "No! I want him!"

I looked at Felipe. He stared right back at me. A great time, I felt like saying, to let me be the boss. "All right. Maybe it's, ah, distinctive that way."

Felipe rolled his eyes but turned on his supplemental lighting.

"See," Sandra said, as if she had never stopped talking, "what you have to understand is I'm going to get out of the life when I get enough money together to go to school."

"What do you want to study?"

"I want to go into archaeology. I always thought that would be the most interesting thing—how people lived so long ago that everything was *completely* different.

"But, see, the other thing you need to know is that I haven't really saved anything yet. The money kind of just goes on—on things."

I knew she meant cocaine. It was certainly her biggest expense, that and clothes.

"So I have to really start now. I have to start saving in earnest. But it's difficult."

"Tell me about your customers."

"Oh, the clients are all kind. There's—I don't know where to begin. There's the ones who want to be nice. But they'll keep after you to tell them things about yourself. How did you get into this line of work? How do you like them? They want to think you like them a lot. Most of 'em don't exactly say it in so many words, but they want you to say they're the best lover you ever had. Smart girls say so, or pretty near. You can get some really good extra tips that way. Plus, the customers, they want to hear your life story. But, see—they don't really want to hear bad stuff, a hard-luck story just brings them down, so you have to make up something funny, or you go, 'Just doin' this while I get my astrophysics degree.' Like that.

"Or they want you to tell them your real name. We go by sort of stage names, but they want you to tell them your real name, because that means to him that you like him better than all the other men."

"Do some of them cause problems?"

"Well, there's what we call troubleshooters."

"What?"

"Mmm. That's a little joke we have. Um—let's see. Problems. We get so many. Well, for instance, there's men who figure you said two hundred dollars for an hour, so while you're in the bathroom showering they turn back your watch. So they get more time and you charge them for an hour. Then you get outdoors and all of a sudden you think it's eleven-thirty and everybody else thinks it's twelve. So you go"—she laughed—"oh, hell, you been had again."

She thought another couple of seconds. "Some of them, they seem like they truly want to please you, but they just plain don't know how. It's like they're childish. Know what I mean? Some regular customers, or even some you've never met, they'll bring presents for you. Perfume or candy or whatever. And sometimes they'll hide the presents in the room and have you start hunting for them. And they'll say, 'You're getting warmer' or 'You're getting colder.' And naturally you're thinking you were already tired, you gotta go maybe three other places tonight, couldn't he just hand the present to you, if he wants to be so nice?"

"Why do you suppose they don't realize?"

"I wondered a lot about that. See, I think it's like this. To them it's an event. The evening. They want to make it special somehow. Maybe they don't get away from home that often. Or nobody listens to them at home. What they don't think about is it's a special event for them. It's not special for me."

"Is there much danger?"

"Danger! Oh—" She giggled, and yet it was a sad sound, meaning that I'd asked a foolish question.

"Danger? All the time I've been in this—been working for this escort service, all I hear from the other women is what to watch out for. How to tell if a guy's gonna cut you. How they've been beaten, or how some guy tried to burn them with his cigarette."

"What about you?"

"Me? Oh." She stopped a moment to put it in a full sentence. "Men sometimes want to hit you. Or, like, pretend to rape you. That's one of the reasons you always have to carry extra panty hose. They rip it. They—you know, it makes them feel good. It makes them feel strong. You can't let it go too far, because, see, you don't know when they're going to lose control. That's why I never let them tie me up. I told the service, they ask for that, you get a different girl. Not me. No way, José.

"Of course, you're going to some guy's room when you go on an assignment. You go to the door and knock—you just don't ever know who's gonna be behind that door."

She paused. I waited. Sometimes you lose momentum in an interview when you don't follow up on a question, but sometimes you get the best material. She had that thousand-yard stare, like she was still picturing events in the past.

"You're best off going to hotels," she said. "'Cause if you go to their own houses or apartments or whatever, there might not be anybody around if you call for help. Hotels, there usually is. Somebody who'll hear you scream. See, I always tell our office manager I don't like to go to homes. But after all, sometimes if business is slow, you just have to. Sometimes the tourist industry is down. You can't be too—if you're too choosy, you may not get work."

She seemed to have come to the end of that topic. Thinking she had talked quite a while without a break, I said, "Sandra, I just realized, I still have the Sacher torte John brought last night. Would you like a cake break? We can always go back to it."

"Let's finish first."

"Whatever you say."

She smiled. She had not smiled very much all day. It was a particularly nice smile, and one that appeared natural for her. "If I eat something too sweet right now," she said, "my voice will get all sticky."

"Sweets to the sweet! Sweets to the sweet!" LJ said loudly, from her shoulder.

"Oh, my God!" Sandra burst into tears again.

Now what? "Sandra, are you okay? Shall we stop?"

"No. No." She swiped at her eyes with the back of her hand. "That's not what upset me. Would you believe I know where that's from?"

"What's from?"

"Sweets to the sweet! It's from *Hamlet.* It's where the queen throws flowers into Ophelia's grave!"

"How do you know that?"

"A hooker who knows Shakespeare is kinda funny, huh?"

"I didn't mean that! I just asked—"

"We did *Hamlet*—my school did *Hamlet*—when I was in ninth grade. I mean, I didn't have any major part. The seniors had the big parts. I was a court lady." She eyed me. "That was the last time I was a lady, too. Is that what you're thinking?"

"No. It's *not* what I'm thinking."

"Prove it. What are you thinking, then?"

"I'm thinking I'm sad. What happened to you after that? In school?"

"Why? What difference does it make?"

"You asked me what I was thinking—"

"I dropped out! That's what happened!"

"When?"

"Early senior year."

"Why?"

"Oh, I don't know."

"Sandra, can't you tell me? Were you a good student?"

"Sometimes. I was good at what I liked. Isn't that the way with most people? I liked English. I hated math, except for geometry, for some reason. I loved drawing the diagrams and proving stuff with the theorems. It was just so great when you could prove a new thing from what you had before."

I gave her a few seconds, but she didn't go on. "And then you just dropped out of school?"

"Well, not *just!* Shit! It was—it wasn't *just* anything. My mother died."

"Oh. Oh, I'm so sorry. What did she die of?"

"She died of being killed. By my father!"

"Jeez!" Felipe was blinking. Then he stopped blinking and looked at me, his eyes wide. But he kept on taping.

"She ... they were always fighting. No, *he* was always fighting." Sandra was not crying now; she was far more angry than sad.

"Go on."

"He'd come home. He was a, you know, a claims adjuster. And he'd stop by a bar after work where we lived in Hegewisch, and then he'd come home, and he'd be pissed, and she'd say something, like, dinner was ready two hours ago, and he'd hit her. Then he'd kind of get into it and hit her a few more times for good measure. Well, I mean, she wasn't a complete fool. After a while when he'd come home drunk she wouldn't say anything. So he'd go, 'I know what you're thinking!' And he'd hit her for what she was thinking.''

"Go on."

"So one time—did I say we lived in a house? One time he was going to hit her and she ran away, up the stairs. So he chased her, and when he got to the top of the stairs, he caught her. And he was going to hit her; he sort of threw a punch and she went over backward down the stairs, and she fell wrong, on her neck somehow, and she died. We didn't have carpet on the stairs. I bet if my father hadn't've been so cheap, and we had carpet on the stairs, my mother wouldn't've died.''

"Oh, Lord. Was he arrested?"

"No. Why would he be?"

"For murder. Or homicide, manslaughter, whatever."

"How could anybody arrest him? There wasn't any evidence.''

"Well, you saw the fight, didn't you?"

Silence.

"Sandra? Didn't you?"

"Yeah." She fidgeted around. "Yeah, I did. But my Dad, the great George Lupica, said if I told anybody he'd say I had a grudge against him. And he'd say I was an uncontrollable child, and they'd put me in a home of some kind and I couldn't go out or do anything there, it was like jail he said.''

"And you believed him?"

"Yeah. I still do. It was true."

Well, she wasn't far wrong. Pretty often kids running away from homes like that, and families like that, got "jailed." Sometimes it was better than home, too. And sometimes it was worse.

"Then what happened?"

"Oh, I started getting uncontrollable anyway." She laughed. "I stayed with friends a lot and then I came downtown and stayed with some friends awhile and then got this job."

EIGHT

"WHO WERE THESE FRIENDS?"

"Oh, just some people I met."

I knew we were getting away from the full-sentence-answer some of the time here, but it seemed more important to keep going. "Met where?"

"Um—the Greyhound bus station."

"Jeez, Sandra! That's one of the most dangerous—"

"Well, okay! I know that! And I knew these weren't the nicest people either, okay?"

"Well, then why—"

"I wanted to get back at my goddamn father, that's why! He's a bastard! He deserved it!"

"He deserved it? But what's happened has happened to you, not him."

"Well, it's pissed him off good, too, see? I mean, here he is with his dumb religion and his lame talk and his rules, and if he ever paid any attention to 'do unto others' I sure as shit don't know about it! And it worked! He was so furious he put his fist through the sliding door, Mrs. Hartig told me. He hadda go to our family doctor, Dr. Wachstein, and get it put in a cast, and I hope it crippled up his knuckles for the rest of his life, which I hope isn't long, okay? You want me to tell it like it is, okay?"

When she came to the end of this, she just sat and stared at me. Slowly, I nodded. We stared at each other a few seconds, and finally I said, "Thank you." I meant it.

And the door buzzer buzzed.

It was Ross. No problem seeing *him* from up here. He had his big, combative face pressed up against the glass pane. Thank goodness he hadn't arrived earlier.

I hurried down and opened the front door. Behind Ross was another, younger man.

"Wait here half a minute. I'll get my coat and be right down." I didn't want him running into Sandra. Especially not while she was getting over an emotional outburst.

"Oh, hell, no. We'll come up and wait."

"Um—"

But he was already three steps up and going forward. That was Ross for you. Sensitivity to nuance was not his strong suit.

I hadn't locked the door, because Sandra and Felipe were inside. As I reached out to open it, Ross just burst in.

"Well, lookit what we got here," he said. In a few seconds, either he'd utter an insult or Sandra would cower away from him. The best I could do now was to get him out of there.

Five people and a parrot is more than my living room can comfortably hold, and Ross was like two or three people, all by himself. As Ross bulled his way across the room, his elbow grazed one of Felipe's lights, which started to tip over. Felipe grabbed it, folded it up fast, reflector first, then tripod, to get it out of harm's way. Then he hurried over to the wall and folded up the other one.

Meanwhile, Ross jerked his thumb at the kid with him and said, "Look what they dumped on me. Name's Gavin."

Gavin was a nice-looking young man, about twenty-five or a bit over. On the skinny side, all knuckles, sharp nose, and elbows. He winced at Ross's description of him as a "what," and I thought I'd better try to help out.

"This is Sandra Lupica, Gavin. And this is Felipe Ignacio from Channel Three."

"Hi, all," Gavin said, smiling.

"This here's a hooker," Ross said.

"Oh."

Ross was obviously not going to win the Smooth Guest of the Year award.

Gavin nodded at Sandra. "I'm Gavin Lowenthal. I just went into Vice three weeks ago, so I don't—"

"Guy's a real cherry," Ross snorted. "And here they make him part of the pussy posse."

I gave him a glare and said to Sandra, "We're going out. What do you want to do the rest of today?"

She had watched all this passively. "Is it all right if I stay here?"

"Sure. I have only one extra key. If you need to go out, it's in the drawer under the bathroom sink. I'll put LJ in his cage now. Don't let him out, whatever you do."

"Braaaak!" said LJ. He didn't want to leave Sandra's shoulder. He was being strangely untalkative, which was probably a good thing. I shut him in the cage in my bedroom, saying to him, "You'll thank me for this later," made sure he had water and birdseed, and closed the bedroom door. Usually, when I went out he was all right flying around the house. But Sandra wasn't used to him, and she might leave a door or window open. LJ wouldn't survive loose in Chicago. Not only was it going to get cold soon, but it was a jungle out there.

Felipe was packed and at the door when I came back. Ross had him pinned, though.

"How come they only show the bad stuff? When cops are friendly and all, do you ever see a story on that?"

"I don't write the news," Felipe said.

"Some cop hits a guy been running around with an Uzi, you'd think he was setting fire to the Bill of Rights!"

"I'm a cameraman. I take pictures."

In the living room, Gavin was sitting next to Sandra on the sofa. Despite having been beaten the night before, she was looking very pretty. The ice had reduced the swelling of the lip, although it was bluish, and you couldn't hide those beautiful, delicate bones, the fragile hands, the warm color of her hair.

They were talking so softly that I couldn't hear what they said. Hmm.

FELIPE DREW A DEEP BREATH when he and Ross and Gavin and I got out on the street. Ross said to me, "So basically you're leaving a hooker-addict in charge of your apartment?"

"Please. I don't have anything worth stealing, and even if I had, it's my business."

"There's such a thing as being too dumb to survive."

"I have already had more than enough advice about Sandra. Drop it, Wardon!"

"Oh, *well,* if you're gonna be testy!"

"I don't think she'd steal anything," Gavin said.

"Shit, what do you know, Lowenthal!"

"Hey, I may be new at this—"

"You're too new to have any opinion at all. So just dry up."

During this exchange, Felipe and I were ignored. "Want to come along?" I asked him. He was carrying all his gear, but he had it strapped together on his back and he was a pro; he'd say so if he didn't want to come.

"They'll let me?"

"Who knows? Hang around and don't leave unless Ross throws a fit."

Which took about a minute. As we walked west on Ohio, Ross said to Felipe, "Whaddaya think you're doin'?"

"Coming along."

"Last thing I need dragging around after me is a reporter. Reporters ain't worth a bootful of piss."

"Cat's the reporter. I'm a cameraman."

"Worse! Git!"

Felipe trudged off to the El. "Hey, that wasn't very nice," Gavin said.

"So I'm not a nice guy."

I said, "Jeez, Ross, mellow down."

"All right. All right. It's past four-thirty. When do we eat?"

"Later. Show me something. I've been thinking— most of the hookers we've talked to are young and good-looking. And expensive. But the ones who are doing reasonably well are just the tip of the iceberg. I think I need to get an idea of the range."

"A block in any direction."

"And after that, I'll feed you both."

Ross said, "If you've got the money, honey, I've got the time."

HOWEVER, Ross didn't mellow down.

It was as if the naïveté of Gavin and me combined goaded him. He plunged into the past-the-El-tracks part of the West Loop. This was supposed to be a heavy streetwalker area.

"Where are all the pimps?" I said.

"Just passed two."

I turned around. Didn't see any likely candidates. "Where?"

"Marsala, you're lookin' for Superfly. Wide-brim hat? Platform shoes? Purple velvet jumpsuit? Mondo chains? Right? That's outta style. Nowadays they mostly wear baseball hats on backward and Levi's."

Chastened, I muttered, "Oh."

"Hey, strawberry!" he yelled at a little girl. She had to be fourteen at best, a thin little thing, her eyes ringed with blue eyeshadow.

She said, "Got something for me?"

"You got ID?"

"Hey, you're a cop!" She was either too young or too zonked to have seen he was a cop right away.

He flipped out a notebook. "You been arrested before?"

"Not here."

"What's your name?"

"Denise."

"Where you go to school?"

"I graduated."

"Sure. You from here?"

She didn't answer.

"What state you born in?"

"Chicago."

He flipped the book shut. "I ain't gonna take you in now, kid." She flipped her hair at him. "But you get your ass off the street. I'm coming back this way in an hour, and if I see you, you're goin' to jail."

"Aw, shit. I ain't doin' anything illegal."

He slapped her rump. "I'm not askin' you again."

She ducked into a storefront.

"Looka that," Ross said. The place was a mini-porno movie house. The front window was painted with the words "Adult" "Adult" "Adult" over and over. Behind the words the glass had been painted black, so that the inside would be dark enough for movies. It was an overcast day and getting toward twilight on the street, and I could see a flicker of greenish light through a few scratches in the paint.

"Storefront movies and a whorehouse in the back. Two, three, maybe four little rooms."

"In that little place?"

"I'm talkin' rooms five feet by seven feet. Plywood pallet on a platform with maybe a sheet of foam rubber on top. Fancy places might have a cloth sheet over it."

"Why don't we arrest them?" Gavin said.

"Can't arrest 'em all. You wanta get a team, kid, do it later. Two people for the front, two for the back. Two guys to run in yelling 'Freeze!' Sure." He swung on Gavin. "But right now I'm *teachin'* you. Got it?"

"Yeah."

"Know why I called her 'strawberry'?" he asked me.

"No."

"A strawberry trades sex for drugs."

I said, "You mean she doesn't even get *paid?*"

"That's what I said, Marsala."

"Hell. I want to talk to her."

"I suppose I could root her outta there."

"Not right now. I need Felipe. I wish you hadn't sent him away."

"She ain't gonna talk for the camera."

I smiled at him. The same sarcastic grin he'd been using on us for the last hour. "Hey, Ross! How about if I
pay her?"

He snapped around and gave me a nod of something
like respect. "Now that just might get her attention."

"According to you, I could probably find her back
here some other night."

"More'n likely."

"She's got to be the lowest paid of all, wouldn't you
think?"

"Except for the yea-number of girls who fu—who
trade sex for food."

Gavin said, "That shouldn't *ever* happen in the United
States!"

"Where've you *been*, Lowenthal?"

"Hey! I may have just been transferred to Vice, but I
been a police officer for six years!"

"Spent all your time ticketing cars? Directing traffic
on Michigan Avenue?"

"No! I was six months on a tac team—"

"Wow! And now you know everything!"

"Plus, I'm getting my degree nights from Northwestern."

"Degree? What the hell for?"

"'Cause all I had was a high school diploma."

"That's what most cops have!"

"Not the new breed. The new breed of police officer
often has a college degree. Two people in my class at the
Academy had graduate degrees. One was a lawyer and
one was an economist. I couldn't afford to go to college, but now I'm taking one three-hour class every
Monday night and in nine years I'll—"

Gavin had not watched Ross's face as it swelled up at
Gavin's words.

"Lowenthal, you moron! A stupid degree ain't gonna help you, you asshole! No degree ever kept any cop from being shot! You gotta go out on the street and get your feet wet with the shit that—"

"Now, that's not what the superintendent said. He said we should pursue more education."

"Oh, forget it! Come on in here."

Ross ducked into a storefront bar. The windows had accordion metal guards and the entry door was steel, but the hulk manning the door let him in without question. If you wondered where all the smokers went in this day of smokeless restaurants, smokeless bars, and smokeless offices, this was the place. The air looked thick enough to cut in blocks and use to package china. The room couldn't have been forty feet across. But the far side disappeared in blue haze.

Ross grabbed a table and said, "Sit there." We sat.

A waiter came over. My guess was that usually the service was much slower, but the owners wanted to get Ross and his weird group out of here as soon as possible.

"Three bourbons, *neat*," Ross said, emphasizing the word.

Gavin said, "Gee, I really prefer beer."

"You're out with me, you do as I say."

"Wardon, I don't have to take this—"

"Pull your chair up to the table!"

"What?"

"Just do as I say. You too, Marsala."

We did. There were several women circulating in the gloom. They wore spangly material, which helped us to see them in the shadows, and wide-net stockings, the kind that were like coarse fishnet. Music boomed in the air, loud but not deafening. There was no stage show, or if there was, it was on break.

One of the women came to our table. "Hi, guys," she said. She ran her fingers over Gavin's hair. "Want me to sit down?"

Ross said, "No, dear."

"Well, why not?" Gavin said.

"We could talk," I added.

"No, dear! Move it!"

"Maybe later, Ross baby." She patted Ross's shoulder, but carefully, like she was patting a partially tame bear. At the same moment, the drinks arrived.

"Pay, Marsala," Ross said.

I paid.

Gavin had been steaming. "Listen, Wardon. There wasn't any reason to get so nasty with her. Plus, Cat here is interested in talking with these women. You could at least have let her sit down." Gavin sipped his bourbon and made a face.

"Heh! Heh!" Ross swallowed his bourbon in a gulp. "Wanta know what I saved you from? You're a sophisticated graduate of six months on a big strong tac team? Huh?"

"Yeah!"

"Plus working on your college degree, huh?"

"All right, all right. What?"

"This is a bar where they give heat."

I saw Gavin struggling not to ask what that meant. He wanted to know, but he didn't want to show that he was ignorant. In my line of work, though, acting ignorant and asking dumb questions is a long-run excellent policy, the very basis of success. While Gavin casually sipped his drink, I said, "What does that mean?"

"They sit on your lap and piss on you."

"They what?"

"You heard me. Some people get off on bein' pissed on. That's why I had you pull your chairs up to the table. That's why I said we didn't want her to sit down. I shoulda let hero here go ahead. Only then he'da had to pay her for it."

Gavin was staring. I didn't blame him. "That's what this bar is *for?*"

"Oh, yeah. They also serve urine in the drinks, if you ask for it." He gestured with his drink. "Like, if this was one, they'd call it a sports bourbon."

Gavin choked on his sip, coughed, and sprayed bourbon all over the table. His eyes bugged out and his face went red.

"Not *these* drinks, you asshole!" Ross shouted, mopping at his shirt front. "I told 'em bourbon neat!"

BACK ON THE STREET, Gavin finally got himself together enough to ask, "Would they have done it, knowing we're cops?"

"They know I'm a cop. What they think about you, I don't know."

"But would they?"

"It's not exactly illegal. Girl can always say she had an unfortunate accident."

I was still not sure whether to laugh or cry. "You know, if you think about it from the point of view of the customer—what is he like, somebody who actually goes out to a bar and pays to have somebody urinate on him?" I started laughing, my brain having apparently decided on its own, without consulting me, to deal with this hysterically. "Guy who wants that has got to have had a very strange childhood."

Ross snorted. "Buncha damn perverts! Oughta lock 'em all up and throw away the key."

"Ross, I don't believe you mean that. This isn't vicious. It's sad!"

See, it's not as if I'm trying for the Miss Naive of the Year award. I know where babies come from and all that. I was told way back in kindergarten about all that stuff and I distinctly remember thinking it was a particularly nasty and ill-conceived method. Ill-conceived! How subtly the mind works, playing little word games on its owner.

The point is, I realize that there is a lot of behavior in the world that is unpleasant to me. But my view is that people get that way for a reason. I wanted to find out more about it, not have Ross dismiss the people as creeps that didn't even deserve thought.

"Hey, Ross. You admit these people are people, right?"

"Not exactly, Marsala. You fuzzy-minded do-gooders don't realize what hookers are really like. Those girls are *not like you.*"

"They're human beings."

"Listen, Marsala. You are a functioning, apparently moral member of society. I don't say I like reporters, but you do your job and you go to work every day and you lead a respectable life, as far as I can see. These people are like stuff under rocks. They aren't doing anything for anybody and they spread disease and make the city look bad. They're like pus."

Whoooo.

The city was on its approach path to the evening, and this section of town was lighting up. Ross had told me about men picking up hookers before going home after work, and I was alert to this early-evening activity as I wouldn't have been a week ago. There were cars with a man or two in them driving slowly, eyeballing the crowds. When a Chicago driver voluntarily drives slowly, you know something strange is going on.

We passed a black woman in a red-and-white-plaid body suit, and she was slender enough to get away with it. Her hair was tipped with silver glitter. A white woman with red hair and black lipstick was being chatted up by a potential customer. There were Thai women, Mexican women, Chinese women, Slavic women, and they were wearing furs, or rags, or Lycra with glittering disks, plunging necklines, rising hemlines, slit skirts, no skirts, see-through lace. Rings!—big glittering rings, hologram rings, earrings like snowflakes, earrings like Gila monsters, three earrings in one ear, and silver, gold, and ruby nose rings. Unlike the pricier hotel call girls, subtlety wasn't big, but there was even a little bit of that, women with mid-length skirts and just a peep of lace at the neck. The two or three subtle ones were actually the more beautiful women, so I deduced they thought they could get away with it. They probably charged more, too.

I said, "Ross, on this street even I can tell who's who."

"Yeah. You're an expert," he grumped.

Gavin said, "Why don't we arrest these hookers? Why are we just watchin' them walk past?"

"Oh, jeez. You could charter a Chicago bus and go up the street picking up one after another of these ladies. Like picking apples. One after the other. Get a busload of fifty, sixty, take 'em in to the district, spend the next twenty hours processing 'em, go out, get another load. Never end."

I said, "Well, which ones do you arrest, then?"

"Organized stuff, when you can. People who run them. Pimps who run big stables. Guys who run big houses or big phone operations. When you can."

"And?"

"Any of 'em who cause disturbances. In the wrong places. Like, near the Federal Building. Like that."

I moseyed along between Gavin and Ross, keeping them apart and watching the passing human parade. It was lively, or maybe it was sad. It's all in how you look at things, of course. Men called to women from cars, and the women went over and leaned in the car windows. The men would be all bright-eyed, like shoppers in a glittery mall. They'd run down their power windows and talk with the woman, sometimes rejecting her appearance or her price, sometimes calling her into the car. The men's faces wore a mix of hunger and a kind of delight at being in control. If you bought it, it had better be what you wanted.

Street pickup is the most dangerous way of all to make money as a hooker. You're out on the street, open to attack. Your pimp hits you if you try to keep any money back. And sometimes he hits you just to make it clear he's the CEO. But he's not out there protecting you every minute, either. He's got other girls in his stable to keep an eye on. So any mugger can come along the street, beat you, and take your money. Or pick you up in his car, rape you, beat you, and then take your money.

You are also prey to the stray crazies who figure they're going to clean up the streets by killing prostitutes, or the other crazies who just hate women. Every age, every city has its roving Jack the Rippers, most of whom either don't kill often enough or don't get press enough to become famous. But ask any hooker if she's known fellow ladies of the night killed in grisly ways, and unless she's very new at the game she'll tell you she has.

And if you are in poor health, if you aren't eating right, and you're out in the rain, and most of all if you're on alcohol or other drugs, then you are also prey to every bacterium and virus known to man. It's not just gonorrhea, syphilis, and AIDS. It's tuberculosis, which is just starting a raging comeback in the underclass and outcasts. And it's good old pneumonia, a plain unglamorous disease that can be overcome by good health, prompt medical care, and clean sheets but runs wild in women skimpily dressed, cold, damp, and malnourished.

The street pickups' life expectancies are not measured in decades, but in years. In some cases, in months.

"They're pitiful, Ross."

"Marsala, you gotta get over the bleeding-heart thinking. These women get into cars they've never seen before and ride around with the men and take the men's private parts into their mouths."

"But, Ross—"

"These are not people! *They are meat!*"

What do I say?

"Ross, take Sandra, for instance. If you look at her, you can see that under other circumstances she could be living a different life."

"She's a hooker!"

Gavin said dreamily, "But she's beautiful, isn't she?"

WE HAD DINNER, which I bought. I was back home by eleven, not late, and I expected to find Sandra awake and bored. I found her missing.

I opened the apartment door with my key, thinking maybe she had put on the chain bolt and I'd have to knock. But the chain bolt was not on. I called, "Sandra?" No answer.

Nobody in the living room. Nobody in the kitchen. The bathroom door was open, and the bathroom dark.

Immediately I raced into the bedroom, to check on LJ. If that damned woman had let him out she was going to be stir-fried in Crisco!

But LJ was fine. Furious, but physically okay. Now I felt guilty about doubting Sandra. She had left to go do something, which was her business, and she had not let LJ out. It was wrong of me to think she might have. She liked LJ.

"*Yaaak!*" he said. Then he imitated the shower, which he sometimes does. "Wishhhhhshhh. Glurpglurple."

So she had showered. After that marathon bubble bath this morning!

LJ and I walked into the kitchen to see if I needed anything else to eat. Which I should not. No. Not after the steak dinner I had bought for Ross and Gavin and me.

Casually, I checked on the smallish cache of mad money—emergency money, really—which I left in an empty cardboard Morton Salt container with a hole in the bottom.

It was empty!

When it rains, it pours.

I'd trusted her. Damn Sandra! Damndamndamn.

NINE

I STOOD THERE with the salt container in my left hand. There was the hole in the bottom. And inside—nothing. No matter whether I shook it or probed around with my fingers.

Had I really believed I knew everything about Sandra? Just because of one brief, tearful soul-baring, which might have been fake anyhow?

No, I wasn't quite that naive. But I definitely had thought she was scared enough to stay here and keep a low profile. Wrong again.

I managed to assuage my hurt feelings with one of the leftover bagels and a good covering of cream cheese. LJ helped himself to a small portion of bagel. He does not eat cream cheese or any other sort of cheese. Just as we were finishing, there was the sound of a key in the lock.

"Sandra!"

"Um, well, yeah. It's me."

"Close the door."

She did. She could see I was angry. "What's up?"

"You've been stealing my money."

"Well, it was right there—"

"It wasn't right there. You had to search for it."

"Jeez! It was only thirty-five dollars."

"Thirty-seven."

"Thirty-seven, then. Don't make a federal case out of it."

"It'd seem more like a federal case if it was *your* thirty-seven dollars."

"Well, yeah. Okay. I agree. I'm sorry."

"That's just great."

"But I had to go home and get my mail. While nobody was likely to be, you know, hanging around watching for me. I needed bus money."

"Thirty-seven dollars' worth of bus money? The CTA isn't the world's greatest bargain, but you can ride for a month on thirty-seven dollars."

"Um—I have a little of the money left."

"How much?"

Sandra carried a paper bag, from which some clothing peered out coyly. She was bopping a little bit from foot to foot as she rummaged in her pockets. "Uh—five dollars and ten cents."

"Spent nearly thirty-two dollars? I'd say that's taxi fare there and back and two dime bags of coke."

For a couple of seconds, she stared at me. Then she yelled, "Hey! You don't own me! You don't get to tell me what to do!"

"I'm not telling you what to do!"

"Oh, yeah! Well, you're telling me not to buy coke, aren't you?"

"Listen to me and stop acting like a baby! I did *not* tell you not to buy coke! I'd rather you didn't, but I didn't say that. What I did say was that you had no right to use *my* money to buy it. Now, do I have that right or don't I?"

"Oohhhhh," she sighed, on a declining note. She leaned back against the door. She was fading quickly from Tough Sandra to Waif Sandra.

The buzzer from the downstairs door started making a racket, but didn't stop, the way it did normally, when somebody just gave it a push. Somebody was pushing it and not letting up. Then somebody started shouting. I could hear the buzzer buzzing in my downstairs neighbor's place, too. Whoever was doing this might have been leaning on all the buzzers in the building. I couldn't tell what he was shouting, but Sandra said, "Oh, no! Oh, my God, he must've followed me!"

"Who?"

"Ohhhh!"

It was one of her disasters, trailing in her wake. I grabbed her hand and started downstairs. "Never mind. Let's go deal with him before he wakes up everybody in the building." My landlord already didn't like me. I didn't need any more trouble.

Sandra pulled back, saying, "No, I don't want to. I don't want to see him," but I was more determined than she was. I whipped the front door open, almost knocking whoever it was down the steps.

Next instant, I wished I had.

A giant hand pushed me sideways and I fell onto the cement wall that ran down along our steps like a kind of railing. Sandra was screaming, "Dad! Stop that! Stop it! Stop it, please!" over and over, until he grabbed at her neck, missed, but got her shirt front and pulled. Sandra fell onto the steps.

He kicked at her, lying there.

She rolled down the steps, away from him, and stood up cowering on the sidewalk at the bottom.

"Whore! You're a goddamn whore!"

This was precisely accurate, of course. But that wasn't the point. The man was in a rage; veins like roots clutched at his temples, and his face was reddish purple in the streetlight. He leaped down and cuffed at her with the back of his hand, as if she were too dirty to touch with his palms. They were big, fast sweeps with his arms held at full length, and the first one caught the top of her head an inch or so above the ear.

By now I had jumped down to the sidewalk, too.

I saw her eyes cross and get out of focus. She reeled. Somehow she stayed on her feet, which was unfortunate, because the next blow caught her on the other side of the head. She made a plaintive sound like a chirping bird and went down.

He drew back his foot to kick her.

Instead, I kicked him, full force on his kneecap, with the toe of my boot.

He sucked in air with a whistle and came for me.

His hands closed around my throat. I tried to pull them off, but his arms were so much stronger than mine that I was ridiculously outclassed.

Red light was flashing in little points before my eyes. But this was one type of attack I had rehearsed for. I wasn't big, I wasn't strong, and I wasn't particularly athletic, but I was sneaky.

I folded my knees, squatting suddenly, and my hundred and fifteen pounds pulled him forward. His head loomed over me.

I sprang up.

My head connected with his chin. Heads are hard. Chins are fragile, and any blow to the chin resonates through the teeth, nose, and up into the brain.

As luck would have it, he must have had his tongue between his teeth, too.

He lurched back, clapping his hands over his face. Blood ran out between his fingers. Hot dog! The maneuver worked! Way to go, baby!

Blood was trickling down his wrist, between black hairs on the back of his arm. When he took his hands away from his face, blood ran down his chin like he was a satiated vampire. "You hurt me!" His tongue didn't work right, but the words were understandable.

"You bet I did! Get out of here!"

"You *hurt* me! I'm hurt! Christ, I'm hurt!"

"You bet you are! You'd better go to an emergency room. You may need stitches."

He got crafty. "I'll sue you! I may have serious damage. I'll sue!"

"You kidding? You pitiful moron! You got two counts of battery and attempted murder here. You hang around another three seconds and I'll call the police!"

"I'll call the police."

"*Do!* Do it from over there! They've got a pay phone." I pointed to a deli in the middle of the next block.

"Aaaah! I'm bleeding!"

"And a sweeter sight I've never seen! Your three seconds are up!"

By now Sandra was on her feet. She said, "Cat! We'd better help him."

"Dammit, Sandra! He's not going to bleed to death! Unfortunately." To him I said, "Move!" He started shambling away.

Sandra said, "Shouldn't we do something?"

"Sandra, do you always change your mind after he beats you? You do what you want, but I'm going back inside." I yelled after him. *"Let me so much as see you around here and the cops'll be on you like flies on a turd!"* Well, it wasn't elegant, but I was mad. I stomped into the house.

The two or three passersby who had hung around at a safe distance to watch the fun decided the show was over. They trooped off reluctantly.

Sandra was staring after him. Then she turned, hoping to follow me inside.

I said, "Come on. Let him clot."

"WHAT AM I GONNA DO with you?"

She grinned, with one side of her mouth. She knew I wasn't going to throw her out. The other side of her mouth remained sober. Her eyes were at half mast. My guess was she was coming down from her coke high. That plus the exhaustion of dealing with her father—adrenaline rush followed by the letdown—had her drooping every which way.

It was too bad. It had looked briefly like she was really trying to give the stuff up.

"All right," I said. "Let's get to bed and worry about it in the morning. But tonight you make up the sofa yourself."

TEN

WHAT WAS LEFT OF THE BAGELS in the morning—just one, with poppyseeds—wasn't as warm and fragrant and seductively delicious as it had been yesterday. But the coffee cake was made almost entirely of preservatives, dough conditioners, dough improvers, sugar, salt, fruit pectin, food coloring, baking soda, and sodium-silico-aluminate, so it was still as "fresh" as yesterday. It would still be fresh when I was in an old-age home or the Cubs won the pennant, whichever came last.

I warmed it, which made it glutinous but tastier. And I scrambled four eggs. This is much more breakfast than I usually eat or usually have time for. But I knew Sandra would come padding in when she smelled food. And I was cooking to avoid making a decision. It seemed cruel to throw her out. But what was I to do about her? This was Friday, September eleventh, six days to air time, and I was running scared. It would be stupid to spend a lot of precious time bolstering Sandra. She'd given me a good interview, but it would still be stupid.

I poured hot water into the Chemex, dished out the eggs, and there was Sandra.

Tentatively, she said, "Hi."

"Hi. Come on. I'm not mad. Have some eggs?"

She split the eggs, half to my plate, half to hers. She cut off a slice of coffee cake and took a bite.

"Mmmmmm!" she said. Which made me feel sorry for her all over again. It was *not* "mmm!" cake. But probably nobody ever made or even warmed breakfast for her.

Since my word processor was using up all the space on the kitchen table, we took the breakfast into the living room and sat together on the sofa. She had already turned on the television set.

BRYANT GUMBEL gave the hand-over to the local affiliates. "We'll be coming back, right after a station break."

Transparent letters whirled into view Frisbee-style against a backdrop of the Chicago skyline. The letters raised themselves up flat to the plane of the TV screen, revealing them to be what was currently being called SuperThree, my channel. They dissolved to reveal Bunny Peyton.

"Good morning," she said, bright as a button, even though she must have had to get up at five o'clock. "September is showing its usual Chicago face. The temperature may drop as much as thirty degrees tonight, from a high yesterday of eighty-two, if a projected front comes through the area. Then again, meterologist John Lloyd tells us, it may not. More about that in a minute."

An inset box appeared next to her head, and I recognized the vestibule outside the City Council chamber. Peyton said, "At a heated debate in the City Council last evening, the so-called Sinless Seven declared that they intended to force a vote on their proposed ordinance to get prostitutes off the city streets." A group of men, five of them solemn, two angry, came out the door. "Other aldermen see this as a publicity stunt, claiming that the ordinances are already in place that would deal with the problem. Garnett Lee reports from City Hall."

"Hey! That's the guy!" Sandra said.

"Which guy?"

"That guy—oh. He's gone."

The screen had switched to Garnett Lee standing alone in front of city hall, clutching a microphone. "Several pivotal aldermen claim that the efforts of the so-called Sinless Seven are aimed at publicity, rather than civic improvement. They say that the ordinances are already in place that would deal with the problem—"

Does one writer do the whole show? I wondered. I said to Sandra, "Which guy was what?"

"That guy on the screen. The one with the dark hair? He comes around to the office."

"What? To your office? To the—"

"The Beau Monde office. Yeah."

"He's a customer? One of the Sinless Seven?"

"Yeah. Well, maybe. He picked up a package there once. I only saw him once."

"Picked up a package—" My antennae were up. "Which one was he? Do you know his name?"

"No. Uh—no."

We finished our breakfast and I clicked off the TV. Sandra said, "I'd like to call Celine, let her know where I am."

"Sure. Go ahead."

This is a small apartment. I could hear Sandra's end of the conversation, even though I was in the bathroom washing my face. Also, since it's my apartment, I'll listen to whatever I darn well want.

"Well, tell them I'm sick and I'll come back to work when I'm better."

Pause while Celine objected, probably.

"Then tell them my Dad hit me and they don't want me to work with a big, huge, ugly bruise on my face."

Sandra's bruise was really not noticeable anymore. As a matter of fact, she was looking beautiful. She had put on just a little bit of makeup—not as much as yesterday—and it was obvious that Beautiful Sandra was emerging from Waif Sandra.

She said to Celine: "Well, between you and me, I'm kind of thinking of giving it up. Well, I know they paid the damned bond, and they can just be as angry as they want. They have to pay bond for us—it's their part of the deal."

She listened, briefly.

"No, no, I know. Christ, I don't have ten cents saved! Well, I didn't mean it that way! Anyhow—"

At about this point, I decided to brush my teeth and missed the rest of the conversation. When I got back to the living room, Sandra said, "Is it okay if Celine comes over? Maybe tonight?"

"Well—" If I said yes, I was tacitly approving Sandra's staying here at least another night. "Oh, sure. Why not?"

"Great!"

"You want to call her back?"

Sandra at least had the grace to grin lopsidedly. "I already told her she could."

Sandra was also going to her room sometime during the day to get her mail. This mail obsession of hers—

"Are you worrying about the AIDS test?" I asked.

"Well, no. Not worried exactly."

"Do you use, ah, protection?"

"Sometimes."

"What does that mean?"

"Well, without, we charge more."

"Oh, spiffy! Swell! That's just wonderful!"

The phone rang. I picked it up. It was a man, asking for Sandra. Since it wasn't her father's voice, I handed her the phone.

"Gavin!" she said.

I went and talked with LJ so as not to listen too obviously. But I might as well not have bothered. Sandra said, "Sure! Half an hour. Sure!" into the phone and hung up.

"He's taking me to brunch."

"Who? Gavin?"

"Yeah. He goes on duty or whatever they call it at noon today, so we have plenty of time. I'll go home after to get my mail."

"Brunch, huh?"

"Mmm-mmm."

"That's nice."

"It's a real date."

"Sandra, we just ate. Eggs. Coffee cake. You're going to eat again in just half an hour?"

"Sure."

How nice it must be to be nineteen.

"Well, I'm going out for most of the day. I have to interview some people and I've definitely got to get to the library while I have a chance. And Ross is coming by at about ten or so tonight to take me to a whorehouse." For now, she could keep the money she'd taken from me.

She stared at me with a look that was either quizzical or outright amused. "You lead a kind of odd life," she said finally.

"I think *you* lead a kind of odd life."

A second passed and then we both started laughing. We laughed until we howled. I'm not quite sure why—we were in a way such strange people to each other. But it was a moment of true mutual sympathy in the middle of a very estranged world. I gave her a hug, and then got up.

"Time to go out and fight the new day," I said.

"Better believe it."

I DID FOUR HOURS of library work, the part of my job I like least, and by three o'clock in the afternoon I was very seriously fed up with books and statistical abstracts. A chili burger at Hermione's café helped. So did several cups of coffee. Hermione had bought a Dalmatian puppy and wanted to bring him over and introduce him to me. I had to tell her I was tied up for a few days.

At a little past four, I decided to stop by and see McCoo. This time of day, he'd usually cleared his desk.

Actually he would have cleared it several times and it would have filled back up several times.

"MC COO, why did they give me Ross Wardon?"

"I asked Cleary that. He said, and I quote, 'The man's not pretty, but he's knowledgeable.'"

"He may be knowledgeable, but he's a troglodyte. He's like every male-chauvinist-pig joke you've ever heard, brought to life in porky-pink technicolor."

"Plus, he's had a few excessive force complaints. Most of them weren't sustained. One was."

"He hits people?"

"Cat, you realize that a lot of the people a police officer is trying to arrest—"

"—are hopped up on drugs, or drunk, or just plain mean. And they don't stay quiet just 'cause you ask them nicely. And even when you've handcuffed them, they'll butt you in the face with their head and kick you. Yes, I know all that. And I sympathize. Really. Still, you people yourselves make distinctions between what's enough force and what's unnecessary."

"Yeah. Well, Wardon's a rough diamond. Got a little macho problem. He tends to get into beefs with his partners, too. But he's been keeping his nose clean lately. And the point is, Cleary gave you somebody who can get you what you want. Right?"

"I'll say. Ross got me an interview with a top-of-the-line hooker I'd never have been able to meet on my own. Plus a lot of reality training, so I probably won't say anything embarrassingly naive."

"He's been in Vice twenty-two years. When he tells you something works this way—"

"—then something works that way."

"He'll keep you from making any naive mistakes. After all, here it is your first television outing, your debut, Cat. Lots of people watching you. I would imagine you don't want to put your foot in it. Mmmm?"

McCoo seemed tense. He didn't lounge back in his swivel chair. This was not exactly Harold McCoo as I knew him. Finally I said, "You're looking a little iffy, McCoo. Is there any—ah—any—"

"Any bad news about Susanne? No, not exactly *bad*. Compared to how bad it could be."

"What, then?"

"She's having a lot of nausea and vomiting from the chemo. She's losing a lot of weight."

"I'm sorry."

"Plus, it's making her feel—I guess the best word is despondent. She acts like she doesn't care about anything anymore."

"Marijuana."

"What?"

"The most effective thing for relieving nausea from chemotherapy is marijuana. And it's *really* effective. I did an article on it for *Medical Update* last year."

"But it's illegal!"

"Yes and no. There's a pill. It's called Marinol, and it's a synthetic form of the active ingredient, THC. That's tetrahydrocannabinol."

"We can get this?"

"Doctors in Illinois are allowed to prescribe it."

"Great!" He was pulling over a notepad.

"However—" I said.

"However what?"

"Well, most doctors agree that marijuana, smoked, is a lot better at relieving nausea than the synthetic pills. To paraphrase the old ad, four out of five doctors who advise cannabis recommended the natural form."

"Can they prescribe that?"

"Doctors? They can prescribe it, in Illinois, but if you take a prescription for marijuana to a drugstore, they won't have any."

"So what do people do?"

"Well, frankly, McCoo, you would go out on the street and buy some."

"Are you kidding? I'm a police officer! I'm an example to people. Plus, I have to be an example to the troops. I can't go do something like that."

"It's your call."

"I'm not naive, Cat. It's not that I couldn't find somebody who knew where to get it."

"Sure. You could find somebody on almost any street corner."

He stared at his desk for a few seconds. "Jeez! I hate to say it this way"—he looked embarrassed—"but what if somebody found out?"

"Hey. Don't ask me. You're a grown-up. You decide."

He nodded, but suddenly I was feeling bad. This was not "Uncle Harold" talking to me anymore, but a friend who was hurting. "McCoo?"

"Yeah, Cat."

"Sometimes I let my desire for a flip remark get away from me. You do have a problem, and it's real, and it's important, and I wish I could help you. I've been thinking a lot the last few days about under what circumstances people are right to give up certain values because of other needs. When are they prostituting themselves for money, or career advantages, or love? I haven't really figured out anything—"

"I suppose it isn't the kind of thing you figure out for somebody else, anyhow."

"No. And it probably isn't right to criticize another person's choice, either."

"She's so...essential to me. You know?"

"Go with your heart, McCoo."

AT SIX P.M., by appointment, I met Felipe at Elm and Sedgwick, where we were going to interview a streetwalker. We started talking with her about six, six-thirty.

What frustration. We plied the woman with hamburgers and Coke. We talked. She talked. We filmed. We fed her more burgers and a chocolate shake.

She was a skinny little thing, jittery, wearing a leopard-print short-short-short skirt. Her hair was tipped orange. She ate like a teenage basketball player.

And it wasn't that she didn't talk. What she gave us just wasn't usable. For one thing, every third word was bleepable. Her vocabulary consisted of "he goes," the F-word, the S-word, "twenty bucks," and "crap."

After a while I was so frustrated that I held the camera and had Felipe try to talk with her, on the theory that she must talk better with men than with women. Not true, however. A new word appeared in her vocabulary. She called Felipe "runt" over and over, apparently as a term of endearment. He was *not* amused. Felipe isn't very tall, but he's hefty and has the muscles of a six-and-a-half-foot linebacker on a five-foot-six-inch frame. No fat at all. I certainly wouldn't want to insult him.

Apparently, this was a woman who didn't actually talk much with her clients.

By nine I was ready to pack it in. We thanked her. Then we cut over to Chestnut to get a cup of coffee.

"You should pardon the expression after all this, Cat," said Felipe, "but shit!"

"You can say that again."

"What now?"

"Tomorrow we have to find the streetwalker I met when I was out with Ross. She ducked into a storefront, and I think we could catch her there. We've gotta have an actual street hostess for balance. We can't just do the expensive call-girl types."

"Okay. Phone me when you've got it lined up."

"Okay."

"But, Cat?"

"What?"

"You're cutting this awfully close. We gotta do the intro and the voiceover. You could really get jammed up."

We parted at LaSalle, both exhausted. I hoped he didn't think I didn't know what I was doing. He'd be right, but I hoped he didn't think it. It was darn clear he felt the evening's work had been wasted.

I dragged on home, thoroughly wiped out. People who think reporters just "write up a few things" and get paid have another think coming.

IT WAS ABOUT TEN when I got off the El near home. As I came within a block of the apartment, I could see the *whip-whip* of Mars lights flashing off walls and windows. Probably not anything to do with me, and anyhow, my problem was what to do with Sandra.

The police cars were not in front of my building. There were three units, and they were at the mouth of an alley half a block down, one nosed in sharply to the curb. For a few seconds I thought of just going on home, but this disturbance was too close for comfort and I wanted to see what it was.

Two uniformed officers were shooing passersby away, and a man in plain clothes but clearly in a position of authority—everything about him said "cop"—was gesturing to a woman in a long coat. She had a flashlight and a notepad and something said "police" about her, too.

I pushed up as close as I could.

The alley, like a lot of them around here, was old brick pavement that had been spottily patched over with tar. The delivery doors of the buildings opened onto a kind of cracked sidewalk, and a shallow curb divided this from the brick/tar alley.

Next to one of the doors, her feet near the door and head toward the alley, lay Sandra. She wore the glittery green top, which sparkled when the cop hit it with his flashlight beam. Her chestnut hair hung silkily back from her forehead over the edge of the curb and trailed into a little dirty water that ran along the gutter. Her eyes stared up at the sky. They didn't blink when the light swept over them.

ELEVEN

A CROWD WAS ALREADY accumulating around the edge of the scene, quiet and not pushy in the presence of death. One of the younger uniformed guys went to his trunk, coming out with a large roll of yellow plastic barrier tape. He tied one end around a telephone pole near the far side of the alley mouth, then backed up slowly, playing the tape out until he came to a parking meter at the curb on Franklin. He went around the meter pole twice, ducking under the tape he was playing out. When it was tight, he headed toward the next parking meter. Soon that whole area of the sidewalk on the main street would be off limits, plus the alley behind.

Then I saw Gavin. He was wringing his hands and moaning, "Oh, no." He was standing near the building on the other side of the alley, leaning against the wall. The crowd was murmuring, but quietly enough so that I could hear him. As I watched, he crossed his arms over his chest and hit his head against the wall. And again. He didn't hit the wall hard; he was not trying to injure himself. But the despair behind the gesture was very evident.

There was no need for me to stare at Sandra's body. I felt too sad. The *whip-whip-whip* strobe effect of the Mars lights combined with the darting flashlight to make the night surreal. I edged toward Gavin. At the same time, the older uniformed cop approached him. "Hey, go get a cup of coffee or something, huh?"

Gavin shook his head but didn't answer.

"Gavin?" I said.

"Huh? Cat. Did you see?"

"Yeah."

"How could this happen? I just don't understand. How could this happen?"

He had to have seen a lot of things like this that happened in the city. But there was no point in telling him so. Maybe for the first time, suddenly, it was personal.

"How long have you been here, Gavin?"

"I don't know. Ten minutes."

"Did you find her?"

"No. That guy did."

There was a middle-aged, slender man in a trench coat and highly polished shoes talking with one of the plainclothes officers. The man held a silky golden retriever on a leash.

"I think the dog found her first."

By now maybe fifty curious citizens were standing around, watching quietly, never mind it was ten o'clock at night. This area is not a night-spot part of town, but it's walking distance from some and has its fair share of late-night delis. And the El station is nearby.

"I went to your place and rang the bell and nobody answered. And then I saw the commotion down here—"

"Gavin, you know hookers are in a dangerous line of work. This kind of thing happens."

"No, she wasn't going to do that anymore. And besides, she wouldn't have been out here trolling. She wasn't a streetwalker in the first place, Cat. And she was quitting. She told me so. She promised."

"Maybe something happened. It could be she had a sudden need for money."

"No. I don't believe it. Everything was fine. We were going to go out to dinner."

"Well—" There was nothing helpful to tell him. "I'll be right back."

Sandra's father—damn him! Who else would do this? Who else was violent toward Sandra, specifically toward Sandra? I edged around the crowd looking for him.

When it was clear that he wasn't in the group of people pressed closest to the scene, I worked farther out, up Franklin to the north half a block, then down Franklin to the south half a block. Nobody who looked like him was hanging around. Finally, I went around the block and came up behind, at the other end of the alley, where I turned up a wino with a bottle. He was so sound asleep I couldn't wake him. I headed back around to Franklin.

At the corner, I met Celine.

"What's going on?" she asked. She saw the police cars, the lights, and probably distress on my face, all at the same moment.

How do you tell people bad news like this? My approach is to just tell them, then stand around to help out if necessary. There isn't much point in beating about the bush; it only draws out the agony.

"Sandra's dead."

"What? No. No."

"Over there."

She glanced at the police and the crowd, but she believed me.

"Some trick kill her?" she asked. A fierce anger was coming over her face. She strode toward the place where Sandra lay. She shoved through the crowd until one of the cops stopped her, then stood stock-still and looked for a couple of seconds, then came back to me.

"Goddamn," she said viciously. "Shit! Shit-shit-shit!"

"Yeah, I know."

"That was a person who never once, in her entire life, did *anything to hurt anybody else! Ever!*" Her voice kept rising toward the end of the sentence, and she ended on a high shout that made half the crowd around the crime scene turn and stare. Abruptly, she walked away from me, but she wasn't leaving; she was only stamping around in a circle. "The bastard! The bastard! The bastard!"

I let her do it. Meanwhile, Gavin had heard Celine and came up to me.

"Friend of Sandra's?" Gavin asked me.

"Yeah."

"In the same line of work?"

"Yeah."

"I don't want to talk to anybody. I'm going home. I feel rotten."

"Wait a minute, Gavin. Did you tell the detectives who she was and stuff?"

"Of course. I may be mad enough to eat glass, but I'm still a cop."

"You tell them she'd been staying with me?"

"Of course. Why?"

"That's good. Then I don't have to wait down here. They can come and find me when they want to. If they want to."

"Oh, right."

"Gavin? What do you think happened?" He might not know about Sandra's father, but then again, she might have told him at their brunch this morning. Maybe he could make a connection.

"I don't know. It's just so unfair. She told me this morning she wasn't going to go on, you know. She was taking a break and rethinking her life."

"Yes, but what she told you this morning—"

"Cat, I realize a hooker may not be the most reliable person in the world. But I think she was serious about it for now. If anything—"

"What?"

"If anything, I would think she maybe went into the alley to buy some coke."

"Why would that lead to murder? The last thing any dealer wants to do is kill a customer."

"I don't know. Maybe he sold her something and then made an advance or asked her right out for sex and she rejected him and he got mad."

It sounded distantly possible, but not very probable. Why would a dealer get mad? He's out here selling, not playing out his fantasies. He's in business. Still, these are not predictable people.

Gavin said, "Cat, I gotta go. I don't feel very well."

"Sure."

He had turned to leave when a plainclothes cop shouted, "Lowenthal!"

"Yeah?"

"Is this the woman?"

The guy was obviously one of the detectives. Tall, slender, and giving off an impression of arrogance, he strode toward us.

"Catherine Marsala?"

"Yes."

"You can go, Lowenthal." Gavin sent me a sympathetic shrug and left. The detective said, "My name's Crossley. Detective Sergeant Crossley. This woman Lupica was rooming with you?"

"Not rooming. She came over two nights ago; she said her boyfriend beat her up and she was scared to go home."

"Why come to you?"

"I guess she figured her father would never guess she was here. Because she'd only just met me last—"

I stopped because he was interrupted by another detective. Crossley turned his back on me while the second man talked into his ear. I heard fragments: "—condo on Walton—elderly—the woman's two children—burglary or not, but they've got a lot of paintings—"

Crossley nodded and said, "Two minutes," to the other man. To me he said, "You telling me you didn't know her well?"

"I met her a week ago for the first time."

"When did you get home tonight?"

"I haven't been home yet. I've been out all day, and when I came up the street I saw you people out here."

"This your address and phone?" He flipped back two notebook pages and showed me what he'd written down, probably when he talked with Gavin.

"Yes, that's accurate."

"I'll talk to you later if we need anything." He started to move away.

"That's it?"

"That's it for now. I have a triple homicide just came in. We'll get back to you."

I was preparing to be outraged that he treated Sandra's death as something to walk away from, but in fact the lab was still on the scene, plus two other detectives and a handful of uniforms. It wasn't the Department I didn't like; it was Crossley.

I caught Celine on one go-round of her stamping fit. "Listen. Do you want me to take you in that bar for a brandy or something?"

"I don't know. I don't know."

Somebody clapped me on the back. "Hey, Cat!" It was Ross. "I rang your bell."

"Oh, hell. I forgot. We had an appointment at ten, didn't we?"

"Yup."

"Do you know what's happened?"

"Yeah. When I saw you down here I went and looked. I guess Gavin had already told the guys the particulars."

"Mmm-mm. Yeah." He didn't seem very bent out of shape by Sandra's death.

He said, "Well? We going out tonight?"

This was not a man who was going to win the Sensitivity of the Month award. For a minute I wanted to ream him out, but what would be the point? The fact that I liked Sandra didn't really mean that he had to like her, too. Also, Ross was far past the age when it would be possible for me or anybody else to reform him.

"Ross, with this happening, I just don't feel like going out. Is tomorrow night okay?"

"Yeah. No skin off my butt." He slouched away toward the El.

IT TURNED OUT that I needed something to mellow down as much as Celine did; we just expressed our anger and sadness in different ways. She was more physical; I was more slow burn.

We went up to my apartment. I let Long John Silver out of his cage. He had been cooped up for hours, and yet he sat on his perch and peered out when I opened his cage door. Sometimes he sulks like that when he thinks he's been mistreated. But it wouldn't have been responsible for me to have left him out flying around the house when there was a woman home who might have been zonked out on drugs and could have left a window open. Anyhow, this was not the time to cater to LJ. I went into the kitchen and got Celine and me two fingers of medicinal brandy in glasses—water glasses; I don't own any snifters.

By the time Celine and I got back to the living room, LJ had finished pouting, and he flew in, saying, "Life's but a walking shadow."

Celine's eyes opened wide and she said, "What's that?"

"My parrot. He was passed on to me by a professor who lived downstairs."

"He talks!"

"Incessantly."

About now, I realized for the first time that Celine was beautifully dressed. Shock hits you in funny ways. If somebody had asked half a minute earlier whether she was wearing Levi's or a dress or a Mutant Ninja Turtle outfit, I couldn't have told them. She was wearing a silky burnt-orange shirt and an equally silky cinnamon-brown short skirt and she looked darn good. The only out-of-sync item was the running shoes, which she was wearing to walk to work in. She carried a large bag, and her high heels were probably inside.

"You on your way to the—a date?"

"Yeah."

"Will you go, now?"

"It's not—I'm due someplace at eleven. Sandra said I should stop by here and I figured to say hello and just see how she—" Celine gulped when she realized what she was about to say. But she finished it. "—see how she was doing. Oh, shit!"

She pounded one hand into the palm of the other. Hard. Over and over. "It's just so goddamn *unfair!*"

"I know. You're not the only one who feels that way. As far as I could tell, Sandra seemed like a really gentle person."

"She was. And helpful. She'd give you the shirt off her back. Well, you know, not that exactly, we're different sizes, but there must've been four or five times she loaned me some money to get through a thin time. Actually, I owe her money right now."

"Bet you did the same for her."

"Yeah." She seemed to be happy at this idea. Her face relaxed somewhat. "But more often the other way. I'm kinda—oh, boom and bust, always up and down."

"In what way?"

"Well, I had this guy who liked to go skydiving. And once in a while I'd go along—"

"You went *skydiving?*"

"Yeah. You have to take instructions and all. It was great. But it was pretty expensive. So I'd get behind and Sandra'd advance me something to get me through."

"Skydiving would terrify me."

"That's what Sandra said. Well, it's all in what you like, isn't it?"

It was beginning to look as if Celine, in terms of living her life, was more adventurous than Sandra. But it was Sandra who had been killed.

"Celine, what do you think happened to Sandra?"

"Oh, shit. You know. Somebody wanted her to do something she didn't want to do and he got mad. Or she ran into a nut case. It's all the same, this business." She rubbed her arm over her wet eyes.

"Did she tell you she was thinking of getting out?"

"Yeah." Celine hesitated. "Yea...eaah."

"Why the hesitation?"

"She'd said it before. Everybody says it. We're all going to get out. Just as soon as we've saved some money. Don't many of us actually wind up breaking it off, though."

We polished off another tot of brandy. Finally, Celine straightened her shoulders. "Can I use your bathroom? My makeup's a mess."

"Sure. It's in there."

She hefted her large bag—too large for a purse, more like a tote, but stylish bronzed leather. She hoofed it over to the bathroom. There was a lot of water running and splashing, then a lot of silence, while I drank just a small extra ration of brandy.

Celine came out looking completely revamped. She must have washed off all of her makeup and started over, changed to gold high heels, even restyled her hair with a hot comb or some such thing. All traces of the tears were gone. She saw that I noticed. "We carry everything we need for repairs, Cat. Us professional women. Didn't you know that? Now, do I look like a million dollars?"

"Sure do."

"Or at least five hundred a night?"

This was a hard kind of humor to accept. "Even that, I guess."

"Don't take it so hard. I know what I'm doing."

"Didn't Sandra think she knew what she was doing?"

"I'm not so sure. Sandra—Sandra was trying to cope. She was just toughing it out a lot of the time."

"Aren't you?"

"Not exactly. Maybe for me it's the thrill."

"What thrill?"

"The excitement. The forbidden. Sometimes I think I get off on the risk."

AFTER CELINE WENT OUT into the night, her head high, bronze bag swinging back and forth, heels clicking on the stairs, the apartment felt empty. Of course, it was really Sandra's absence, after two days of dealing with her and her problems, that made the difference. As I picked up the glasses we had drunk our brandy from and finally started looking around the apartment, I suddenly realized that some items were different.

Near the sofa was a pink plastic suitcase with white bands. Sandra's. On the sofa, on top of the blanket she'd been using, was a medium-sized brown paper bag. Sandra had come back here earlier with some of her possessions, then gone back out on the street.

Maybe this was evidence the detectives ought to see. But it wasn't present at the actual crime scene, was it? And it was in my home and therefore could be construed as my property, couldn't it? And anyway I could always tell them about it later, couldn't I?

Inside the suitcase was, of all things, a set of gray flannel pajamas. Also a yellow sweatshirt, several pairs of blue lace underpants, three bras, all sky blue, a toothbrush, a half-used tube of toothpaste, a Dean Koontz novel, a beeper, a pair of Levi's, a pair of shiny silver stretch pants, four emery boards, deodorant, a five-dollar bill, a corner torn out of the *Star* with a horoscope on it and the words for April partly blotted with lipstick: "You will meet new people at work. Be open to new experiences. Old flames may present opportunities, but beware of letting your heart rule your head."

So much for the suitcase. I dumped out the contents of the brown paper bag. Three letters, opened. A Snickers bar. And an even smaller brown paper bag.

I looked at the letters first. One was a bill from Lord & Taylor. $879.21. This woman spent a lot more on clothes than I did.

The second was an appeal to send money to save the redwoods.

The third was from the Department of Health. She had tested positive for the HIV virus.

Oh, my God! I held the paper and reread it three times. Then suddenly I realized that that was probably what Sandra had done. Reread it and hoped the letters would change, hoped it didn't say what she thought it said.

They wanted her to come in for counseling.

Sandra must have opened and read this letter back at her old room, as soon as she saw it had arrived in the mail. She had been watching for it. Then she came here—and what? Left her stuff on the sofa and eventually went back out on the street. Why? To turn a trick and get some money for something? Or did she go out to find some coke to take the pain away and dull the fear?

I got up nervously and went out to the kitchen and boiled some water. It was really just for something to do. Took out a package of herbal tea, poured the water over the tea—and then wondered if this was a cup Sandra had used and was I in any danger?

No, that wasn't the way to think. It was wrong.

But I knew how it felt to have just that creeping doubt. What was safe? What wasn't? Had Sandra bled anyplace around here? When I put the ice on her bruise the first night she came, was she bleeding? I thought not. Did I have any open cuts on my hands? No visible ones, but how could I be sure? What about the towels in the bathroom? What about the sheets? What about anything else she'd used while I wasn't around? Combs? Knives? Razors?

Stop that!

This was no way to behave, with Sandra dead. I was ashamed of myself.

In my mind I believed what the doctors said, that casual contact was no risk. It was just a matter of getting control of my emotions. I took the tea back to the living room, sat on the sofa, and opened the smaller brown paper bag, half expecting to find cocaine.

A lipstick fell out. The color was Strawberry Shortcake. Sandra had been shopping. A sales slip and another thing fell out. For a few seconds I couldn't take in what it was, and turned it over in my hand.

It was a Hartz Mountain cuttlefish bone. A treat for birds.

I started to cry.

TWELVE

NIGHTMARES ARE NOT my thing. Or dreams, either. Maybe I don't dream, or maybe I have dreams and don't remember them. But that night in my mind I walked.

The streets unfolded before me. Down Franklin, from my place, block after block, under the El. There was nobody at all on the street. It was night, and the streets had the Venusian glow of the sodium-vapor lights that have been installed all over town. Except that the light didn't come from actual streetlights on poles but from my eyes.

The El rattled by above. Then another El train and another. I walked block after block in a glow that was the color of pale peaches, but nevertheless cold.

Stores were all closed. The art galleries were closed. The delis were closed. But in the windows of the galleries were twisted, deformed paintings, and the color from them ran down the walls and pooled on the floor—scarlet, midnight blue, and a green the shade of poison plums. In the windows of the delis lay dead chickens and dried fish, smoked chubs and herrings, that looked like they had been washed up onto a beach and had lain in the sun for days. The clothing stores held sets of pants and sweaters and caps, placed on the tilted display panels in the sequence they might take on a body, but there was no body in them, or one that had shriveled down to nothing, liquefied, maybe, and run out through the pores in the fabrics.

I hurried up onto the El platform, because all the people had been sucked out of the stores. And a train rumbled into the station, stopped, opened its doors, and then closed them and started away. There were no people inside it, no passengers, no engineer. Just a few hats and scarves and empty shopping bags.

I wanted desperately to run and find someplace that wouldn't be strange and empty. Someplace normal. But there wasn't any such place. Then I thought of the lake. Lake Michigan would be a source of peace; because it was always a huge expanse of water, was always so big that it dwarfed humans, it would be a source of normalcy and comfort. I bolted down the El stairs, ran east on Chicago Avenue past stores and restaurants. All empty. I crossed Michigan Avenue. Michigan Avenue never slept. And it was brightly lighted even now. But there were no people.

I ran east on Chicago Avenue, past the Northwestern University buildings—the law school, the medical school, the dental school, three major hospitals. There were lights on inside but no moving figures.

I plunged across Lakeshore Drive, nine lanes wide here and all empty, leaped over the cement dividers. No need to dodge cars; there were no cars. Some pieces of clothing had blown up against the guardrails.

The sandy beach was ahead of me. I ran toward the water.

And ran. And ran. Some rusty cans and plastic bottles lay around. There was a wooden hull of a rowboat. Several pieces of concrete. Rotten boards and logs, some pipe, a glass bottle.

Lake Michigan was dry. It wasn't there.

I WOKE UP SHIVERING with cold Saturday morning in a room that felt like a hundred and ten degrees. The dream seemed to have taken hours, and in fact the sky was turning gray in the east. For a few seconds I tried to laugh. How ridiculous! Lake Michigan vanishes! But the horror lingered—the sight of that great, empty, shallow hole where Lake Michigan once was.

Chicago is so centered around the lake that it is almost as fundamental as the subsoil the buildings rest on. The dream was as shocking as if I lived in the shadow of Mount Fuji and then some ordinary day I turned and looked over my shoulder and found it gone.

And yet, there had been no real threat in the dream. No pursuer, no weapons, no injury.

Just loss.

And maybe that was it. Sandra.

Lighten up, Marsala. You're overreacting.

When I stopped to think about it, Sandra had certainly not been a longtime friend. Or even exactly a friend. If anything, she'd been sort of a pest. A pill. A thief, even. A hanger-on. A burden. But the sort of burden that reminded me of Boys Town—she's not heavy, Father, she's my sister.

She left a gap. I truly missed her.

I poured a bowl of cereal, the end of a box. The box had been hiding in my cupboard for months. Most of what came out was broken up pieces and dust. It looked like bird food. I held up a small amount on my palm for LJ. He eyed it with one big, wrinkled eye and said, *"Braaaaak! Yuk!"*

He was right, too.

We sat on the sofa, LJ and I.

The cuttlefish bone Sandra had bought lay on the coffee table in its plastic bag. Should I give it to LJ? Or was it evidence that ought to go to the police?

And then the ideas started to come—thoughts that I'd been too tired or too shocked to grasp firmly last night.

Sandra had certainly not been killed by somebody she bought cocaine from. Pushers did not kill customers. Second, it was not very likely that she was killed by some john, some casual customer she had solicited. Sandra may have been only nineteen, but she was a veteran. She would have been careful who she went into an alley with.

And much, much more important than that, she had just received a positive HIV test. Sandra was a hooker, but she was not an evil person. She just plain *would not* have immediately gone out and chanced infecting somebody else.

Or would she, if she had been angry at all men on earth?

No. Because she wasn't angry at all men, just her father.

What then? Her father. Sandra had come home, come up to the apartment, put her things here on the sofa. Maybe she had started to settle down for the night—no, no, she had invited Celine over. And obviously she was expecting Gavin, too. She'd had brunch with Gavin. At brunch they must have decided to get together after he got off work. And what? Go out with Celine, a threesome?

No, no. Celine couldn't stay long; she had a customer. Sandra had a date with Gavin; she was apparently treating Gavin as a real, genuine date, not a customer. Which was sad, too. As a young girl, with her kind of family, she probably didn't have a lot of chances to really, happily date. And now, when she gets a chance, she dies.

All right. She'd arranged to see Celine and Gavin last evening. Then she goes to her room in the SRO and gets her mail. Reads the horrible letter.

Now—does she want to see Gavin? Or Celine?

Probably she comes back here wanting nothing so much as to hide under a blanket and cry. But Gavin and Celine are coming over anyway. Maybe she'd want to tell Celine. Girl talk. Girl talk for the nineties, at any rate. Celine would sympathize. Celine was a sympathetic sort of person, plus they must both have known women in the game who got AIDS.

So far so good. But Gavin is coming over, too. She'd want to be bright and cheery for him. At least temporarily. Until she decided what to do. How would she handle that?

She'd go out and buy some coke.

I was back to where I had started. She would have quieted the pain with happy dust. That was likely. But still, no pusher would kill her. It had to be that her father had trailed her back here again, or had waited for her here, maybe in the deli, watching for her to come back. And when she did, he rang the doorbell. And Sandra, much as she feared and maybe hated him, nevertheless had that stupid pity for him, too. She wouldn't want him to come up here. He might break things up in the apartment if he got violent.

So she went out to talk with him on the street.

Then what? She would have been at the end of her rope emotionally. Would she have challenged him? Would she have accused him of setting in motion all the family dynamics that were going to kill her?

The cereal tasted terrible. I dumped it down the sink. It would have to be instant coffee for breakfast; Harold McCoo would disown me. Actually, going without calories would do me good. I'd been eating too much on this assignment.

All right. Sandra went out to meet her father.

Her death had to be avenged.

No doubt about it, I would have to talk with the police.

AREA SIX IS A LARGE, tan, bland building surrounded by squad cars. If you go inside and persist long enough to find the detectives' room, you will find yourself in a large, bland room with gray floor tile and bland metal desks. Unlike the film representations of these places, the desks do not have pictures of family on top, or memorabilia like baseballs autographed by favorite players, or hatchets used in a favorite crime, or even stacks of paper, unless the desks are being used. The reason is that detectives do not have particular desks of their own. They come in on their shift, carrying their briefcase and word processor and take whatever desk is free.

The twenty-five district police stations in Chicago are headquarters to patrol officers, youth officers, Vice, beat reps, tactical teams, neighborhood relations, senior citizens' services, and several other functions. They are the first to respond to a crime like Sandra's murder. The area headquarters usually encompass four or five districts. Detectives work out of the area headquarters. Ordinarily they are informed by the district about a violent crime and respond second.

Sandra's body had been found in the Eighteenth District, which is in Area Six. Area Six, located on Belmont and Western, takes in the Eighteenth District, called East Chicago, which starts just south of the Chicago River and goes northward along the lake, including such good stuff as Navy Pier. Area Six also covers four more northerly districts: the Nineteenth (Belmont), which is inland, and the Twenty-third (Town Hall), which lies along the Lake, and then the Twentieth and Twenty-fourth, both of which touch the lake. After that Chicago becomes Evanston and other north suburbs.

So Area Six incorporates a huge part of Chicago, five large districts running north from the center of the city. The Area covers twenty-two square miles. Last year, the districts in Area Six responded to half a million calls for service and reported sixty thousand serious crimes. Put another way, they have their hands full.

They had their hands full without having to take care of me, or walk me through their investigation into Sandra's death, which was what the expression on the face of Detective Benny Crossley was telling me. He didn't say so in words. He was too smooth for that.

Instead, he crossed a nicely creased navy-blue pant leg over another of the same, leaned back in his chair, and waited for me to talk. He was a slick type generally, slender and fit. Fit like a thousand hours at the Nautilus machines.

"Sandra Lupica had been staying with me for a few days. I told you that last night."

"What were you doing taking a hooker into your house?"

My head snapped up. "Why shouldn't I?"

"Do any escort work yourself?"

"I'm not even going to get angry at that. I'm a writer. I met her when I was working on a story for Channel

Three.'' That made him pay attention. ''She needed a safe place to stay.''

''It didn't turn out to be so safe, did it?''

''It might have been, if she'd stayed inside.''

''Hookers don't stay inside.''

''Detective Crossley, are you trying to tell me that you don't want to hear what I've got to say?''

''Not a bit. Thought you wanted to ask questions.''

''I do. I want to give some information and get some.''

''We don't do trades here.''

I had intentionally not asked McCoo to call and tell these guys I was okay. This could always be done later, if necessary. I wanted to find out how they felt about hookers and how they investigated hooker murders, without confusing the picture by having them worrying about the brass.

I said, ''No trade necessary. I'll give you my stuff first. Sandra had come back to my apartment sometime during the late afternoon or evening—probably evening—and left some clothes and other odds and ends before she went out. Including these letters.''

He opened and read all three, stopping longest at the Board of Health letter. Then he tossed them on his desk.

He said, ''Okay.''

''I think she was desperate. Who wouldn't be after reading that? She must have gone out to buy coke. Then she was probably intercepted and killed by her father.''

''Why her father?''

I told him about the attack Thursday night. ''My guess is, he would have intended to beat her, not kill her, but he went too far and hit her too hard. Which leads me to guess that she wasn't shot or stabbed. Nothing premeditated. No weapon. Am I right?''

''Maybe.''

"Oh, come on!"

"The autopsy hasn't been done yet. Today, probably."

"I know that! I'm aware it's too soon for the autopsy. But you still must have seen the injuries."

"All right. I suppose it can't hurt to tell you. She had what looked like a depressed occipital skull fracture. What you would call the base of the skull."

I was going to tell him I knew what "occipital" meant, but why bother? He was having more fun this way.

"And a split lip, a broken tooth, cuts inside the mouth. When we see this, we think that the victim may have been punched in the mouth. The teeth cut the inside of the mouth when the lip is struck. You understand?"

"Perfectly." Any average rocket scientist could figure that out.

"And so we think that she may have been hit with a fist. The blow may have caused her to fall backward and strike her head on the curb. You see how that might happen?"

"If I really cudgel my brains, yes. Any evidence of who it was?"

"No *clues*," he said, smiling.

"How well did you look?"

He stopped smiling. "We did a thorough survey of the area. I don't know what you think, Miss Marsala, but you're barking up the wrong tree. We don't skimp on homicide investigations."

"Even when it's a hooker? Even when you think it was closer to manslaughter than murder? Even when you half think she asked for it?"

He stood up. "Even *anything*. We do our job."

"Well, thank you for your time." I started out. When I got as far as the door and he hadn't called me, I turned back.

"If you're so intent on finding the killer, why didn't you ask me her father's name and where he lived?"

For a couple of seconds, he glared at me, realizing he had made a mistake. Then he picked up a notepad. "Go ahead," he growled.

"George Lupica. Someplace in the Hegewisch area. You can't miss him. He's the man with the cut tongue."

THIRTEEN

I CLEANED LJ'S CAGE. Not my favorite thing, and oddly, not his, either. You'd think he'd like freshening up. Nice new newspaper on the cage bottom. Nice, clean, washed bars where previously he had splattered them up. But for some reason it makes him anxious, and he flies around the place uttering little parrot sounds of dismay. These are a kind of whistling hoot, which people say are the same noises African grays make in the wild when their enemies come around. They have only two enemies, a yellow-filled kite that looks a lot like a falcon, and the vulture eagle, *Gypohierax angolensis*. Other than man, of course. While I cleaned, I gave LJ a hard-boiled egg to keep anxiety at bay. It always seems a little bit like infanticide when LJ eats an egg, but it's probably natural enough in the wild.

Afterward, I rewarded him with a piece of banana. Banana is one of his favorite foods. He eyed it for a second, drawing out his delight. Then he grasped it in one claw, while he stood on the other foot. LJ does this with no loss of balance, or even any appearance of difficulty, and he seems to use either foot equally well.

Polishing off the banana piece, LJ said, "He is well paid that is well satisfied."

He'll quote Shakespeare in preference to any other author.

"Well, I hope you'll stay satisfied awhile, because I have to go out."

He said, *"Braaaak!"*

I had been forcing myself to do housework, trying to let the police do their thing on Sandra's father without horning in. My patience had run out rather quickly—say, forty-five minutes. George Lupica, Sandra's father, was listed in the Chicago phone book on Avenue F, which was far south. I was going to pay him a call.

DRIVING SOUTH into the Hegewisch area was a step back in time. There are lots of Chicago neighborhoods like this, primarily the Eastern European ones—Polish, Serbian, Czech, Bohemian, Hungarian—where time seems frozen in the late 1940s. Many of the women wear head scarves. The men wear astrakhan hats or stocking caps and cloth jackets with knitted shawl collars. The stores were mom-and-pop shops: Stanley's Sausages, Sophie's Flowers, Simon's Fruit and Vegetables. Even the touch of tech-y hype was in its way very old: "Dial the Virgin," a sign said. "Tell the Virgin Mary Your Troubles."

Hegewisch was currently in an uproar over Mayor Daley's plan to build a third Chicago airport (or fourth if you count Meigs, which a lot of people don't because it's so small) at a cost of $10.8 billion. It was the old story. An airport would provide hundreds of new jobs. It would also destroy many businesses by the simple move of turning the lots they were built on into runways. It would be very, very noisy. And it would certainly destroy the character of the neighborhood.

Would contractors make a lot of money? Why, sure. Would any of this splash over onto some politicians? Could be. There was also a lot of hazardous waste from a hundred years of manufacturing on the land where the airport might be; in fact that was another argument—that nobody anywhere had enough money to clean up that much hazardous waste except federal and state money combined on a major project like this. Hazardous waste aside, it was a sure thing that there would be cash waste that trickled down the political patronage pipeline.

Hegewisch is the kind of place where most of the people who live there have always lived there. They all know each other. They know who lives in each house. Which does not mean that they necessarily know what goes on behind the home's closed doors.

The Lupica address was in southeast Hegewisch, not too far from St. Simeon Mirotocivi Serbian Orthodox Church, a landmark with its yellow and red brick set in elaborate patterns. This was maybe twenty blocks south of US Steel. Never mind the twenty blocks, in this area you feel loomed over by US Steel. The Lupica house was on Avenue F, and was almost as far south as you can go and still be in Chicago. It was also just blocks west of the Indiana border. The house was also just blocks from Wolf Lake, the gloomy lagoon where Leopold and Loeb abandoned the body of Bobby Franks.

Leopold also lost his glasses here, an oversight that eventually led the police to the killers.

The Lupica house was a one-story bungalow faced in tan stucco that gave an impression of solidified porridge. The windows were small and the door narrow. It looked mean spirited, but that may have been just an extension of what I knew of the people who lived there.

The bell was not melodious, but a harsh buzzer. There was no window in the front door. Lupica had to open it to see who was there. He flung it open. It bounced off the wall behind.

"Mr. Lupica?"

Now that he could see who I was, he tried to slam it.

"Wait a minute, Mr. Lupica!"

"Get out of here, bitch!" Apparently, his tongue injury hadn't messed up his ability to speak. Pity.

"Hold it! Have you heard what happened to Sandra?"

"I've heard. That fucking police detective came barging in here."

"Crossley?"

"No, some wop named Marconi. Coulda met him, you came ten minutes earlier."

"Anyhow, why shouldn't he barge in here?" Silently I apologized to Crossley for thinking he'd do nothing because Sandra was a hooker. At least he'd promptly sent somebody to check it out.

"He's got no business in my house!"

"Sure he has. It's his job to find out who killed her."

"So? Let him go sniff around those whoremongers who employed her."

"Well, when you come right down to it, who was it who actually threatened her?"

"Threatened her?"

"Yeah! You!"

"I didn't threaten her."

"You sure did. I heard you."

"I didn't threaten her, you stupid bitch! I chastised her!"

"You want to explain the difference?"

"Yeah. I—what I told her was what would happen to her from her whoring around. I told her that God didn't like what she was lettin' herself be."

"Did you kill her?"

"Hell, no."

"Can you prove where you were last night about nine?"

"I was here. Never left the house."

"Alone?"

"Shit, yeah! Nobody else lives here anymore."

Small wonder. So now the cops and I knew he didn't have an alibi. "See, you could have tried to *chastise* her again. Too hard. And she fell and hit her head."

"Well, I didn't." Suddenly he realized that for a few seconds he had been carrying on a conversation almost like a normal human being. And he regretted it. "Hey, what're you doin' hanging around here, anyway? I'm gonna call the police."

I looked at his porky red face, his sweaty, receding hairline. A real cornered pig. We'd done this little dance before. I said, "Yes. That's a good idea."

"I'm gonna do that." He half turned back into the house.

"Good. You do that right now."

He came rushing out of the door at me, bellowing. There were words in the bellow, the way pecans are embedded in fruitcake—swamped and broken—but I got the idea. He didn't like me. I put out my foot, and he fell over it.

"Oh, shit!" he screamed, in a high-pitched whimper. "Why don't you leave me alone!!!? You goddamn dykes! You want everybody's balls!"

He was lying on the sidewalk. "What a sorry specimen you are," I said. "You get your testosterone in an uproar by stepping on everybody else's mind?"

"Bitch!"

"I'm not a lesbian. But people who are aren't taking anything away from you. What the hell's the matter with you, anyway?"

"Die! Just drop dead."

"Sorry. Not this time. If you've heard that Sandra's dead, aren't you sad? You're her father."

"Aahhhhh." He struggled up on all fours, then stood. He wasn't injured.

"She was just nineteen years old! Didn't you wish her a long life?"

He stared at me, now that he was upright, big fleshy folds around his eyes, and the eyes themselves bloodshot. Far inside there, some kind of strange, sick regret shifted position.

"Oh, yeaaahh," he sighed, almost like a breath. "I wished her a long life. If she'da stayed home."

CHICAGO TRAFFIC GIVES YOU two options: gnash your teeth or try to use the time profitably. Not having with me a tape of, for example, instruction on the tenses of Greek verbs, I spent the time thinking about George Lupica. Why did my talk with him bother me?

Because it rang true.

That was an odd reason, in a way, to be distressed, but until then it had seemed extremely likely that he had killed his daughter. Possibly he had not meant to, but if he had killed her as the result of one more fit of abusive rage, it was murder, in my opinion. He'd hit her many times in the past, including day before yesterday, and what was more important, he had been willing to hit her right out on the street in front of other people, the way she had actually been killed. But when he said he had not killed her, it sounded right. Why?

Because of the emotional tone? Yes, possibly that was it. He was exactly the same man he had been two days earlier. There was a small touch of regret in him that Sandra was dead, but most of his old belligerence was intact. And that simply did not spell guilt.

If he had killed Sandra, there would have been a number of things going on emotionally under his surface—self-justification, defensiveness, fear of being found out, possibly even a sense of guilt. And they would have pushed some aspect of his behavior out of line. He would have been much more belligerent than before. Or much more conciliatory, tacitly saying, "See what a nice person I really am?"

But he was exactly right for the innocent man—innocent of killing her, at least. Slightly befuddled, but still angry, nasty, and convinced that he and his worldview were right.

This was not really a welcome conclusion. Because, if her father didn't do it, who was left?

IT WOULDN'T HELP TO ASK Ross Wardon or Gavin Lowenthal to give me inside information about the investigation of Sandra's death. They wouldn't have any inside information. They didn't work out of the same building as the detectives. Detectives sometimes lord it over other officers, and if any detective was going to lord it over other people, Crossley was my candidate for the guy most likely to do it.

I would ask McCoo when I got a chance. I had other problems. Days were running out, and the interviews and backup were not done for the TV essay. This was Saturday. The air date was Thursday. Five days to get it finished—no, actually three. Felipe had said they wanted to look at the "final cut," whatever that was, on Tuesday. No matter how much my sorrow for Sandra hung in my mind, it could be disastrous to waste time trying to avenge her death.

However, with a little guile, cunning, and deceptiveness, a person might be able to combine the two.

It was still *possible* that Sandra's father had killed her. In fact, he was in terms of statistical probability the most likely killer, the one with the most recent and most obvious violent feelings toward her. But while I had been talking with Crossley another thought had come to me.

When Sandra and I were watching the news yesterday morning, she had seen the Sinless Seven. And she had said that one of them came to "the office." What was an antihooker alderman doing in an escort-service office?

I didn't think that customers went to the office. They called on the phone, didn't they? And the service sent somebody to the client's home or a hotel room. A house call.

And if the alderman was not there as a customer, he was there for another reason. What if that other reason was a financial interest? Suppose one of the Sinless Seven owned all or part of an escort service?

Could anything so devious occur in Chicago politics? Does it snow in Canada? Does the CTA ever run late?

Letting my fingers do the walking, I picked up my phone and dialed Beau Monde. A very gentle, soft, feminine voice answered.

"Beau Monde. Companions for every occasion."

"Uh—I'm looking for a job."

Her voice changed to very clipped and businesslike. "Experience?"

"No, uh—no."

"Age?"

"Thir—" Oh, hell. Thirty-five sounded old. From their point of view. "Thirty."

"Really? And you have no experience?"

Ooops. "Look, I just lost my job. I'm a computer programmer. I don't look thirty. I look a lot younger, and what's more, if you have clients who want an escort to take to parties where they have to *talk*, not just wriggle, then I'm perfect for the job. I'm a college graduate and I can hold my own in conversation."

Cooly, she replied, "We already have several of those. However, if you look good, too, it's quite acceptable."

"That's nice."

"You'll have to come in for an evaluation."

No doubt. "I just have one or two questions. First, how much do you pay?"

"I can't tell that until I see you."

"Swell. All right. Second, do customers come there to meet their—un—date or do they just phone?"

"They phone. With their wish list," she added.

"I see."

"Shall we set up an appointment?"

I already had the piece of information I wanted. But curiosity overcame me. "Yes, please."

"Tomorrow. Two P.M."

"On Sunday?"

"You have an objection to Sunday?"

"No. I just thought you'd be closed."

"We never close."

"Right you are."

I thought I'd keep the appointment. It was possible I would even be able to get a lead on which alderman Sandra had recognized.

Because she *had* recognized him. She had fudged it over quickly after speaking, saying impulsively that he was the one with the dark hair, then backing off. But she had seen him, recognized him, and immediately, because she was a smart young woman, guessed what he had been up to.

Then what? She had gone to brunch with Gavin. Okay, how long could that take? Two hours? Gavin,

with Ross, was working two to ten P.M. yesterday. So
Sandra was certainly free after two. She hadn't seen Celine during the day, and if she had gone directly to her
room and then come back here, she would have been
back a long time. If she had been back a long time, there
would have been coffee cups and food wrappers around
the kitchen, or she would have curled up on the sofa,
thrown a blanket over herself, and wept about the HIV
test. There was no evidence of either.

So what had she done?

She had gone to her room in the SRO, picked up the
mail, read the Board of Health letter, and what? Gone
to see her father? I doubted that. Gone to a friend? The
elusive boyfriend? Maybe. How would I find out? Not
easily.

Suppose she had been a little desperate. As well she
might. She opens the letter and thinks, My life is ending. What then? She thinks, The world has used me and
now it's going to destroy me. And she'd be pretty much
right. So where can she turn for something, such as
money, to make the time ahead of her more pleasant?

The alderman. She's seen him on the news and she
knows that he is not what he seems. And also not what
he wants people to think he is. But she may not be sure
of his name. What does she do to find out?

Sandra was smart. She thinks about it. Of course—she
buys a newspaper! The "Sinless Seven" were a major
story. They'd intended to be a big story. There'd probably be a photo with a caption, and she could probably
get his name that way.

She buys a newspaper on the street, then comes back
here, carrying it. I got up and looked in the wastebasket
in the living room. Empty. I looked in the kitchen trash
can. Not empty, but no newspaper. Just crud. I looked

in the bathroom wastebasket. A newspaper! On page three was a photo of the "Sinless Seven."

The names were under the picture: Lon Smith, Clint "Corky" Alvarado, Mustafa Pa, Barry Pintakowski, Bennett Perkins, Fred Holder, and Gene Cirincione. There was no arrow, X, or mark of any kind next to any of the names.

What did Sandra do next? Well, while I like Sandra, she was a lot like Celine had said, a person struggling in a world that frightened and took advantage of her. And she fought back the best way she could—using whatever came to hand. She had most likely come back here in the late afternoon and telephoned the headquarters or home of one of these aldermen. And threatened blackmail.

Blackmail. It might have taken her some time to reach the alderman himself. These are busy people. That might be where a lot of her afternoon went, making phone calls. I might be able to verify later with the phone company where those calls went. When she finally reached the alderman she could have said something like "Meet me at the corner of Franklin and Ohio at nine P.M. with x dollars."

It sounded plausible.

Now I had to figure out which Alderman it was.

FOURTEEN

ROSS WAS SCHEDULED for this evening. Maybe we could find the streetwalker. Whether Gavin would be coming or was too unhappy was yet to be seen. I had plenty to do between now and then.

I had got back home from Hegewisch by noon, already feeling like I'd had a long day. Well, an interview with the cops plus Sandra's father on top of it would do that to you. The answer to this kind of weariness, of course, is food, and Heaven is the place to go.

Hermione's Heaven is not big, but it's bountiful. You want health food, go to Heaven. You want chocolate, go to Heaven. You want ribs, go to Heaven. You want pasta, go to Heaven.

Hermione herself is bountiful. She's never told me what she weighs, but it must be at least three hundred and fifty. And she takes no nonsense about it, either. "I don't ask you to gain weight, you don't ask me to lose" is her motto.

She came toward me, big arms outstretched. "Hey, Cat!"

"Hiya. What's the special today?" She always has one new item. They change every day.

"Today it's the Im-pasta-ble."

"Oh, Herm. That's awful!"

"Big bowl—kind of a trough, really—with three-color linguine, two hot Italian sausages, two big meatballs, roast red peppers, broccoli, onions, garlic, and all the grated romano and parmesan you can put on it."

I simply said, "Yes."

Hermione waited to come over and sit down until I was about half finished with the trough. She's very sensitive that way. She could see that eating came first, then when the inner woman was no longer screaming, friendship came second.

"Hermione, how do you feel about sex?"

"What? Cat, you never ask questions like that!"

"I'm talking philosophically, Herm, not personal secrets. I'm doing a thing for television on prostitutes, and it's playing hell with my feelings."

"You feel sorry for hookers?"

"I started out feeling pity for them. Then I got to the point of feeling sorry, which isn't the same thing. Now I'm feeling sympathy, which is a step further. Not that they're all in the life for the same reasons, but I'm getting to understand how they feel."

"You know the old saying that people who marry for money are just prostitutes with society's blessing?"

"Yes."

"Does this all have anything to do with your long approach/avoidance conflict with John?"

"And John's money? I hope not."

"Oh?"

"It may."

"I don't suppose you can just relate to him as an individual and forget that his family has money?"

"Well, at times I do. Sure. But if I actually married him—I don't know, Hermione. The money I earn would be such a drop in the bucket. I wouldn't feel like I was contributing to the, you know, family endeavor. Plus, John and I don't think exactly the same on everything."

"Do any two people think the same on everything?"

"Well, but would I be compromising? I'm not sure when a person is compromising and when a person is just giving in."

"Eat your broccoli," she said. While I complied, she showed that she'd been thinking about my earlier question. "Sex is a major creator of ambivalence. Take me, for instance. Now there are some people in the world who truly suffer when they see fat people. They figure fat people are hurting their health, in the same way smokers may be hurting their health. I can accept that. But once they know I know the hazards, they oughta let me alone to run my own life."

She was usually not as explicit about this. I listened.

"But there's another group who seem to *fear* fat people, or maybe even hate us. They say vicious things. And I've always thought the reason was that we look kind of like fertility symbols."

She stood up. She was wearing a cherry-red knit shirt and a red-and-white pleated skirt. Hermione did not wear clothes that apologized for her size. She was correct in what she was saying; her breasts were like watermelons, thighs like my whole body, lavish rolling belly between. "See, and it scares them," she said. "I mean, it'd be none of their bloody damn business otherwise, but they feel—not say so, but *feel*—that I'm flaunting it."

"I think you're right."

"And I bet you get the same thing with hookers. Uneasiness. People are frightened of sex."

"Frightened in general?"

"Sure. See, most people don't think they're very good at sex. I mean, how much experience do most people have? They figure they're not so great at it, but they're too uneasy to ask, and maybe they have a few relationships, but when they break up they figure it's because they're no good in bed anyway, or else if they were, the guy thinks he'd have been able to hold on to the woman, or the woman thinks she would have been able to hold on to the man. And the people who *do* have a lot of experience are worried that they're promiscuous and they wonder if that means something is wrong with them, plus their relationships break up, too. So they don't know if they're really any good at it, either."

"Okay."

"And the few major, demented egotists who think they're absolutely great are liable to be dead wrong, so you can leave them out of the reckoning."

"I can see you've thought a lot about this."

"You bet. Then they see these hookers making money—some of 'em making serious money—and it plays right into their insecurities. They figure, These women sure know something I don't. And that's the first step on the road to hatred."

THE REAL PUZZLE, though I didn't tell Hermione, was how Sandra herself felt about sex. Because it seemed to me that the question of who killed her had to do with her attitude toward being a prostitute. Did she feel like a professional who was good at her job and who was getting paid for doing something well that most women do for free? Or did she feel like a victim, whom anybody might as well take advantage of? Or did she feel doomed—somehow preordained to struggle in a job just a few steps above the gutter and die, literally, in the gutter?

It mattered, because all this had to do with what chances she would take, what chances she would not take, when she would fight back, whom she would trust, and whom she would challenge. Why she would have gone out that night, and whom she might have met.

CHANNEL THREE never closes, and Felipe wanted me in ASAP, today or Sunday, to do some rough editing. We were running low on time. The segment would air Thursday, which meant the higher-ups had to view it Wednesday, which meant a damn good rough cut had to be finished on Tuesday. Yes, news departments in television studios are able to produce things extremely fast if they have to, and they often have to, but like everybody else in the world, they'd take time if they could get away with it.

I thought I'd stop by Three today and kill two birds with one stone. Find out how much material we already had and take a look at the place where they would film me.

Felipe was in some sort of photo lab when they called up for him from the desk, but the receptionist said he'd meet me in Studio 2C. I also had her call the office of Mr. Zucrow, the big enchilada of news programming, and if he was in tell him I was in the building, in case, though I didn't put it this way, there was any wisdom he wanted to impart.

Studio 2C was intimidating. It was about a hundred feet square, half of it stage and the other half banked seats rising up much more steeply than an average movie theater. The seats were not plastic, as so many theaters have now, but instead were covered with a very deeply nubby fabric, for sound absorbency, I supposed.

On the stage were several oddly mixed chairs—a wing chair upholstered in dark green, a wood stool, two captain's chairs, and three beat-up metal folding chairs. Several cameras stood around, two with cable attached, all of them looking more like something you'd see in the intensive care or nuclear medicine departments of a hospital than on a stage.

There was a lighted booth high on the wall on my right and a dark booth high on the wall on my left. The lighted booth had enough electro-techno-audio-visual-computer equipment to power the Pentagon.

I was extremely intimidated. When I get intimidated, I immediately decide that *nobody* is going to be able to tell. Basically, I go into my Clint Eastwood mode.

"Hiya!" It was Felipe.

"Hi, Felipe. How does the tape look?"

"Not bad. I'll take you down and show you some of it. Reason I asked you to meet me here in 2C, we're gonna tape your narration here." He studied me. "It always helps if you see the place first. Loosens you up."

"Do I look like I need loosening up?"

"No, no. No. Not at all."

"You're a kindly soul."

"You betcha. When will you have it ready?"

"The intro is done. And I've finally figured out how I want to structure the essay—"

"And how is that, Ms. Marsala?" The Voice of Zucrow spoke, but he was nowhere in sight. Felipe pointed to the lighted booth. Zucrow said, "I'm coming right down."

In thirty seconds he stepped out of a door next to the stage on the same side of the room as the booth.

"You're cutting it close, timewise," he said.

"Not really. We have a lot of material now. And that's been the point of taking some time. Getting a variety of hookers, and ones who were willing to talk."

"I see." This was a very dry, noncommittal man. "So you were saying you knew how you were going to structure the piece. How?"

We were at a decision point. He could shoot down my approach, or okay it, or force me to change my standards and do it his way, or force me to quit. I said, "By the different types, you might call them levels, of prostitution. People don't know how much of a caste system it is. And within the types I want to focus on two topics. First, the economics of prostitution. Which hookers make the most money, which the next most, and so on down, and who really gets it—where the money goes after the hooker accepts it. Second, the hazards. Which kinds of prostitution are the most dangerous, which less dangerous."

"It sounds very—factual." He said "factual" as if that were bad.

"I hope it is *very* factual."

"We need guts. We need blood, sweat, and tears."

"What do you mean?" I was getting tense and a little angry. Felipe wiggled his eyebrows up and down as if to say, Be careful.

"More anguish, more distaste, more emotion."

"Mr. Zucrow. I don't do soap opera and I don't do purple prose. I let the facts tell the story. We've got plenty of facts here."

"You ever heard 'If it bleeds, it leads'?"

"Sure. And I want stories with human content as much as you do. But I don't have to draw the conclusions for the reader. I mean the viewer. Viewers aren't stupid. They can draw their own conclusions. If the facts don't tell the story, you can't do it by editorializing. And if they do, then you don't need editorializing."

"A purist, huh?"

"No. I just have my own way of working. You hired me for a reason, right? And if you don't want my work done my way, you'd better say so now."

He folded his arms. Felipe was staring at both of us, not moving a muscle. There was at least five seconds of total silence.

Zucrow said, "We'll give it a shot."

"Thank you." I was relieved and grateful.

"After all," he said, "you're not under a long contract."

INTENTIONALLY, I did not tell Zucrow about Sandra's interview and death. I just could not bear to use her suffering to increase his ratings. Someday, maybe, I would write about her. Someday when the pain was less.

Afterward, Felipe took me to the lab and showed me how you mark tape so you can take out segments you want to use. It was much, much easier than dealing with film, which I had once upon a time learned to splice. This was all done by machines with digital readouts. The tape remained untouched by human hands. We took a look at the interviews we'd accumulated.

"We have more than enough to fill the time," he said.

"Sure, in total time. Five times what we need. But we're gonna pull just the best remarks. The ones that have to do with the way I want to structure it."

"You can do that easily enough. We've got to sit down and get to it, though."

"That's not the only problem. I want one good representative of every type of hooker. We don't have a streetwalker."

"We have Miss Inarticulate."

"Yeah, and that's the trouble."

"Well, I don't know, Cat. Maybe it says something about the job that we'd have to bleep every third word."

"Mmmm. Maybe. You mean, that's the kind of person who gets stuck at the bottom of the barrel?"

"You betcha."

"Maybe—no, what am I saying? No. I want somebody who can at least tell us one or two memorable streetwalking details. About the money. Getting robbed by her pimp. Or by a customer. I want that! I need that!"

"Ah, the minute they start to think like directors they get temperamental!"

"I'm not temperamental."

He chuckled. He was kidding, I think. I said, "Felipe, is there any way I can look at a certain portion of a recent morning news program?"

"On this channel?"

"Yes."

"You betcha. No problem at all."

I told him the day and the approximate time. After a certain amount of fussing around in another lab, he brought up the local portion of the morning news on a small screen. He fast forwarded. I waited, watching for the "Sinless Seven" to appear, then as they started emerging one by one from the revolving door at City Hall, I tried to remember exactly how we'd been sitting and exactly when Sandra had said—

"There they are!" I said, nearly echoing Sandra.

"Who?"

"One of those two. It was just at that instant Sandra said she recognized one of them. She said the one with the dark hair. But there were two with dark hair coming out the door right then. I'm not sure which she meant."

Either Gene Cirincione or Clint "Corky" Alvarado.

IT SEEMED GAVIN was coming along tonight with Ross and Felipe and me on our tour. When I got home, there was a message on my machine from him that Ross would be a little late, so Gavin would meet me at the Baskin-Robbins ice-cream store on Walton.

"Ross oughta be here in fifteen, twenty minutes," Gavin said when I arrived. He was eating a hot fudge sundae on what looked like pistachio ice cream.

"I know what you're thinking," he said. "But I always eat sugar when I'm depressed. It helps."

"In that case, I'll go get a chocolate cone."

We sat. Gavin did appear to be seriously shaken by Sandra's death. He looked drawn, not like the cheerful young man of two days before.

There was something I had to do, and when you have an unpleasant duty, it's usually better to get it over with. "Gavin, please tell me something. And give me this much trust—I'm asking for a good reason, even if I don't want to say why."

"Well, sure, Cat."

"Did you and Sandra get to the point of having sex?"

"Uh. Um, why do you—oh, well, you said you didn't want to say why. All right. We didn't."

"Thanks." Then I was not morally obligated to tell him about her HIV test.

"It hadn't been going along like that. Our relationship. I think she thought that this was *really* different from her, you know, job. And she was making it different from her job by getting to know me first."

"I can believe that. It was obvious she was dealing with a lot of changes in her view of herself."

"Yeah." He thought a half minute and said, "Hell! She was so sweet, Cat. I think it could've worked."

"What happened to your knuckles?" His right hand was swollen on the knuckles and one was cut.

"Oh, shit. When I got home last night I was so mad I hit the wall."

"Jeez."

"Not very mature of me, huh?"

"Understandable."

We ate for a while. Finally I asked, "When's Ross gonna get here?"

"Any minute, I guess. Lucky us."

It was said so bitterly I had to ask, "Don't you like Ross?"

"No, I don't like Ross. He's a—a caveman."

"Oh, he just puts on a macho exterior. He's okay underneath."

"Cat, you have a dangerous tendency to think the best of everybody."

"I don't either! I'm very realistic."

"He says terrible things about women."

Probably about Sandra, and Gavin took exception. "Oh, I know that. But Ross is just kidding."

"No, he's not. He really means the cruddy things he says."

Felipe turned up then. With Ross's permission, Felipe was going to come along. I had nagged, wheedled, and begged to get Ross to agree to this. Time was too short for me to line somebody up for an interview and then go back later with Felipe and find the quarry was gone. Felipe had a hand-held camera slung over one shoulder and a couple of rechargeable lights in a bag slung over the other. I had the releases for people to sign in my pocket. First we'd hunt, later we'd eat.

Ross arrived. I think he was getting accustomed to free meals. He was less crabby than usual.

"I've got an appointment with an escort service tomorrow, Ross," I told him.

"For what?"

"Well, they think I'm looking for a job." It was for the essay, to an extent; it was also to look for the alderman, but he didn't need to know that.

"Watch yourself," Ross said.

"Shouldn't be a problem. I'll look and then get cold feet. I was thinking after that I might try one of those embassy-row whorehouses we saw the first time we went out."

"You mean ask them for a job? Are you crazy, Marsala?"

"Why? It's not dangerous. I'll just back off before things go too far."

"I don't mean that! They won't look at you twice! Marsala, for those places, you have to be knockout, drop-dead gorgeous!"

WE DIDN'T FIND the streetwalker I wanted, or any other streetwalker.

We hit a cheap whorehouse. Not the cheapest, storefront variety, but medium cheap, a hundred to two hundred dollars per, according to Ross. I don't know what Ross had on these people, either, but they let us film the halls and rooms, without any people in them. My ideas of whorehouses must have been formed by movies, probably movies about the 1890s. I expected red flocked wallpaper, Victorian furniture, and gloom. Well, today it's Mylar, chrome, and stereo music.

"Aren't you worried the camera will jiggle?" I asked Felipe as we trekked up a Mylar-papered stairwell. I was carrying the lights.

"You betcha it'll jiggle," he said. "What we got here is gonna be cinema verité."

FIFTEEN

"IN 1911, five women out of every thousand in the United States were prostitutes," I said. "In 1990 it was two of every thousand. Prostitution, while no more prevalent, seems always with us." Felipe had all the studio lights on. It was so bright and so hot that I wouldn't have to go to Cancún this year, which was a good thing, since I couldn't afford it anyway.

"Few people realize, however, that prostitution today has quite a rigid caste system, based on the beauty, youth, and to a certain extent the social presentability of the women.

"Lowest on the ladder are the streetwalkers, who may trade sex for money or even for drugs, and who will go with men to the men's rooms or get into cars with them. The streetwalker usually has a pimp, and the pimp usually takes most of the money the streetwalker makes. Because they go to unknown destinations and get into unknown men's cars and are out on dangerous streets late at night, theirs is the most dangerous end of the profession, as well as the lowest paid."

We would decide later whether to intercut these introductions with the women talking, or whether to run the whole intro first and then do the women, one after another. I was leaning slightly toward the second, thinking it had more impact to see the women all at once, one after the other. But we'd get this taping done now. Because it was early Sunday morning, the Channel Three building was less busy than usual. Which was a relief.

We had the studio as long as we wanted it, and there were no spectators.

"Next up the ladder are the women you may see working bars in restaurants or hotels, often called bar girls or B-girls. They also may belong to a pimp's 'stable,' but a lot of them are freelancers. The freelancers keep what money they get, but they lose whatever slight protection there may be from having a pimp around watching over them."

I described the other levels—whorehouses, call girls, the by-reference-only, briefly. Then I said, "Let's let the women speak about their lives."

Felipe killed some of the lights.

"Was that all right?"

"It was fine, Cat. Why wouldn't it be?"

"Oh, I don't know. It seemed like half the time I was mumbling and the other half I was using pedantically precise diction."

"You weren't. That's just jitters. Now I'd like to do those other bits. Just pause a little after each part, and we'll decide where they go when we cut and paste."

"If you say so."

I took a resolute breath. He turned on the lights. I said, "There were eighteen thousand prostitution arrests made last year in the city of Chicago. These women may have gone to jail overnight before seeing a judge. But of those eighteen thousand, only ten—not ten thousand, ten—served any time in jail beyond that first detention.

"Some critics of the system find these figures alarming. However, in these days of overcrowded prisons, it is a difficult question for society to deal with— does Chicago really want to jail more prostitutes?"

I paused.

"Today, prostitutes are ravaged not only by the historic venereal diseases, but also by drugs, and now, of course, by AIDS. Most of them think they will remain prostitutes only long enough to make enough money to go into a legitimate line of work. Few do. Few get out of the business until they simply become too old to be marketable, and then they have no job skills. Many do not make it out of the life alive."

I paused again.

"In 1985 the executive director of the Chicago Crime Commission stated that prostitution was 'destroying the city.' But the city goes on. It is probably more accurate to say that prostitution is destroying the women who get involved in it."

IT TOOK ME A WHILE after leaving Channel Three to get rid of the adrenaline generated by the challenge of looking and sounding like a reasonable human being while talking to a videocamera and thinking the piece would eventually be seen by several hundred thousand people. An early lunch of a Polish hot dog with extra relish and extra mustard followed by a brisk twenty-block walk home helped a lot.

After a play period for LJ, which involved rolling his Nerf ball along the floor and letting him sweep down and kill it, I phoned McCoo at the Big Cop Shop. He answered.

"What are you doing there on a Sunday?" I asked.

"Why are you calling me if you don't expect me to be here?"

"I'm calling in case you're there."

"Why are—never mind. What do you want?"

"I've got a request and a tip. And a question."

"Forge ahead, Cat."

"The question: How is Susanne?"

"Actually, she's better. Your, uh, suggestion was helpful."

"Mmm-mm. Good. My request: Can you tell me the autopsy results on a Sandra Lupica? She was found dead in the Eighteenth on Thursday night."

"Lemme see if I can get that. It should've hit the files by now." He rummaged while he talked. "We are going to have this all on a database someday. Pull it right up on a screen. Someday soon, I hope. But not soon enough—aha. I've got it."

"Would you be willing to tell me the cause of death?" Some cases he will, some cases he won't.

"Trauma to the brain. Looks like she was struck twice on the chin and mouth and then probably hit the back of her head when she fell against a curb or some such. Friend of yours?"

"Yes." Nobody had ever exactly asked that, but it felt pleasant to say it. "Any other interesting stuff?"

"Cocaine in the nasopharynx."

"Oh. I was afraid of that."

"And now. You were going to give me my reward."

"What?" I was thinking of Sandra. She'd been hit twice. That made it different, less accidental.

"A tip. Remember?"

"Oh, yes. You've heard of the escort service Beau Monde?"

"No, but I don't doubt it exists."

"Well, you've heard of the 'Sinless Seven'?" There was a snort from his end, so I continued. "I'm pretty sure either Corky Alvarado or Gene Cirincione of the Sinless Seven is part owner of Beau Monde."

"Really? My, my, my! Now, *that's* interesting."

"It's also possible Sandra was blackmailing which-ever it is. And so it's also possible he may have killed her to shut her up."

"I'll pass that along."

"And later today I may find out which one of them it is."

"Cat! Whatever wild idea you have, don't do it! Don't get involved. I can pass this on to Vice and they can in-vestigate it the safe way."

"I won't do anything unsafe. All I need is some background for a story. You know me; I'm always care-ful."

BEAU MONDE WAS LOCATED in moderately high-rent land on East Walton. There are very expensive apart-ment buildings along this street, plus such tony shop-ping as Bloomingdale's and Armani.

The address was an office building faced with glossy pink granite. Inside, a first-floor receptionist sat at a curving white desk. She was a slender, attractive black woman with extremely long carmine fingernails. "May I help you?" she said when I walked in off the street.

"Beau Monde?"

"Your name?"

"Sue Duncan." That was the name I'd decided to use. "I called yesterday."

Did she look at me *meaningfully?* Maybe I was just self-conscious. She reached forward and pressed a but-ton on her console, carefully using just the pad of her index finger, with the nail held so it wouldn't be dam-aged. She could never have run a word processor with nails like that.

"Beau Monde?" said the speakerphone.

"Sue Duncan to see you."

"Send her up."

"Fifth floor, Suite 5K," she said.

"Thank you." Nobody was getting in this building without being detected. She probably had a call button for a guard on the console someplace.

Beau Monde was a small office, just a reception room and another adjoining room, from which wafted a smell of coffee. The tones were beige and white. "Ms. Duncan?" said a sharp-featured woman at the desk, clearly the person Sandra had called the office manager. I recognized the voice as the one that had spoken to me on the phone.

"Yes." I reached out to shake hands. She touched my hand briefly and reluctantly, I thought. I was already feeling vaguely unclean, and this added to the sensation.

"I'm Mrs. Gordon."

Mrs. Gorgon was more likely, one of the mythological sisters who had sharp claws, snakes for hair, and whose look turned people to stone.

She placed a sheet of paper on her desk, squarely between the Rolodex and the phone, and took down my name, address, phone number, and Social Security number—all hastily fabricated. Then, glancing back and forth between me and the sheet of paper, made some other notes without asking.

"You can work evenings? Nights late?"

"Yes, I'm still looking for a computer-programming job days."

"If you do well for us, you may not need it."

"Oh. Well, that's wonderful. Are we required to engage in sex with the customers?" After all, wouldn't most people ask?

"Absolutely not. We are not a front for, um, prostitution. Your conduct with the client is your own business."

"I see. How much do I get paid?"

"I'd start you out at four hundred a date, of which we take sixty percent."

"I see."

"And I'll see how you do."

"On-the-job training?"

She didn't respond to that. "One of our young women named Lainie is in the waiting room. She'll give you some coffee and answer any questions you might have."

"All right." I got up and went into the room she pointed out, the room the coffee smell came from.

Lainie set me straight. She was a doll-like creature, very small, with straight, dark hair cut Chinese fashion. She offered me coffee, from a percolator pot set on a hot plate. When I shook my head, she drew me over to a pair of chairs as far away from the door as possible, and she spoke in a lowered voice.

"You haven't done this before, have you?"

"No."

"I could tell. I can always tell."

"You can?"

"Always. Now, what I'm supposed to do is tell you the *real* facts. See, that makes it possible for the witch to say she never asks any girl to have sex with a customer. But you gotta, of course. Or you'd never make any money. Well, hardly ever. There's gay guys sometimes who want you to go to a party with them for...to look like—"

"Camouflage?"

"Right! And then once in a while, somebody really does want a just-plain escort. But not very often."

"So usually—"

"Usually you gotta go to bed with them."

"Oh."

"Now, you'll have a credit-card stamp with you. That's okay. And cash is okay. You can take tips, but if they offer cash, don't tell them the price is more than the witch quoted to the guy, because she'll find out. She gets real mad real easy. And don't take less than she quoted. She'll tell you before she sends you out what you're supposed to be paid."

"I see. And no checks?"

I was kidding, but she said, "You can take checks if you're careful, like, if she's already okayed it. In-town clients the witch'll mostly know about anyhow, so they will have been good for the money before. But most of the guys will be out-of-towners in hotels, and you should take a look around. If they're genuine, sometimes a check is okay. Like, if they're associated with a major corporation. The witch'll know that, too. Usually you take cash or a credit card."

"How do I know if he's a cop?"

"Check him out. There oughta be a suitcase, if he's a legit traveler. Look in the bathroom and see if he's got a shaver laid out, some shaving lotion, like that. If you're really suspicious, ask to see his airline tickets and his car rental papers."

"Couldn't cops bring stuff like that?"

"They don't usually bother. I'll tell you the dead giveaway that it's a cop."

"What?"

"Take-out sandwiches and plastic coffee cups!"

SHE GAVE ME SEVERAL other hints. Like, turn off your beeper before you go into the room. It makes a bad impression if it goes off at the wrong time. Take a shower afterward, but don't spray yourself down with perfume. It's a dead giveaway to hotel security. If you want the biggest tips in this kind of high-class operation, don't wear loud clothes. Go in wearing something a bit prim, maybe even gloves and a hat. Lace around the neckline is good. For some reason, men love to think you're a proper lady.

She also explained that the results of the first couple of "dates" would tell the Gorgon what she could charge for me as time went on. She'd probably try me on a couple of regular customers first and get detailed reports.

By this time, I was feeling thoroughly soiled. And I wasn't even intending to go through with it. Was this how Sandra had felt all along?

"Well, thanks. I certainly appreciate the...um, tips." Through the door I could see the Gorgon, sitting at her desk. Guarding the Rolodex and the computer. Was there any way to get rid of her?

"Oh, you're welcome," Lainie was saying. "We oughta stick together anyhow. I mean, I sometimes think the amount they take—I make eighteen hundred dollars some nights and she takes twelve hundred of it—" Her voice fell to a whisper, and the head of the manager rose simultaneously, as if scenting revolt. Maybe I could pit them against each other in some way.

"Well, I gotta go," Lainie said hastily.

"Say, is there a bathroom here?"

"Little girl's room is right there." She pointed at a door I had thought was a closet, next to the table with the coffee and hot plate.

"Thanks. Well, 'bye."

"'Bye." I opened the bathroom door, but Lainie was leaving, waving good-bye to the Gorgon. I picked up the coffeepot, went into the bathroom, and poured all but a film of coffee down the sink. Then I came out, put it back on the hot plate, and turned the dial to high.

I crossed into the reception area. "Thanks," I said to the Gorgon. She looked at me carefully, as if to find out whether Lainie's "introduction to the business" had upset me.

"You'll hear from us," she said.

"I have just a couple of questions—" I began. The coffee started to burn.

The Gorgon was sniffing the air. "What's that?"

"Something's burning," I said helpfully.

"Shit! The coffeepot!"

She jumped up and ran into the side room. Immediately, I leaned over the computer. How could I get into the data base in half a minute? From the other room came curses, followed by "Shit! Lainie—brains of a gnat!—shit!—ouch!"

The computer was impossible. It would take an hour to figure out the access code. I swung the Rolodex around and flipped fast. A—Al—Allen—Alvin. No Clint Alvarado. C—Canfield—Cindy—Cirincione. Aha! Gene Cirincione. Just an address and phone number. Quickly I found another male number. It was John Canfield, with an address and phone number, and also the notation "blondes, short, big b." That, obviously, was a card for a customer. Which meant Cirincione's card probably wasn't.

The water in the bathroom stopped running. I swung the Rolodex back, after flipping it to where it had been, at A.

"Sorry," the Gorgon said. "Lainie is a sweet girl, but not very technical-minded. Now, can I give you any other information? We'd like to give you a try. We'll have a beeper ready for you next time you come in. You'll understand, of course, that we can't pay you quite as highly as we would if you were ten years younger." She smiled widely and viciously as she said this.

"I quite understand. I'll be in touch. I've got all the information I need for now."

SIXTEEN

THE ELEVATOR DOORS opened just as I was about to punch the down button. Celine got out.

"Cat!"

"Shhh!" I waved my hands. The door to Beau Monde was open, but it was forty feet back down the hall, and there wasn't much likelihood that the Gorgon would hear what we were saying if we kept our voices down.

"What are you doing here?" Celine whispered.

"I'll tell you about it. Let's go someplace." I gestured toward the elevator.

"I gotta get my paycheck. I'm *totally* out of money."

"Okay. I'll wait here."

She came back stuffing her check into her large handbag.

"Let's go to Starbuck's," I said. "I'll buy you a coffee."

STARBUCK'S HAS CHICAGO'S closest approach to San Francisco coffee. Someday I would have to ask Harold McCoo, chief coffee brewer of the CPD, whether he approved of Starbuck's. Probably not. When it came to coffee, McCoo approved only of himself.

We sat at a tiny table, which made us lean close to each other, though I suspect we would have anyway, in order to talk softly.

"So what were you doing there?" she asked.

"Trying to find out more about the job. And Sandra."

"Isn't Ma Gordon horrible?"

"She certainly is. Celine, can I ask you more about Sandra?"

"Sure. Why not?"

"Well, I know it's kind of personal—"

"Hey. *No problem.*"

"I didn't get the feeling Sandra's attitude toward her job was the same as yours. You're sort of a free spirit, and Sandra was sad—almost tormented."

"Sandra," Celine said quietly, "felt like she was doomed. Doomed. And this job was the best she could do with her life. Like she would never go any further."

"But do you think that feeling of being doomed would push her to take chances?"

"No. Sandra didn't like taking chances. In a funny way, she was *very* cautious and conservative. I'm telling you, she thought this was the *best* she could do. This job meant stability for her."

"Would she have been different—would she have gone wild if she found out she had HIV?"

Celine's mouth dropped open. For a long, long time she couldn't speak. This had to be the horror that all women in her position shared, if they were sensible enough to think about the future at all.

"She had AIDS?" Celine whispered.

"No, but she had the virus."

"She knew?"

"She'd just found out. That day."

"Ohhhh. Oh, no."

"Would that have driven her to take a risk?"

"Sandra would just have burrowed into a hole. She'd have tried to—you knew she did some coke?"

"Yes."

"That's what she would have done."

"I agree."

"You knew she got it at the deli near you?"

"No! There's a dealer there?"

"Yeah. She told me on the phone."

"Do you do coke, Celine?"

"Naw." She grinned. "Matter of fact, almost all white hookers are on drugs. But a lot of black hookers aren't."

"So backing up, you're saying she wouldn't have been out on the street turning some street trick to get cash."

"Absolutely never. See—Sandra was basically an expensive call girl. More expensive than me. For her to just go out on the street and, like, give head for twenty dollars would be like, say, a brain surgeon decides to just run out and do a—a foot massage!"

"Okay. I can understand that. It's still very difficult to understand who could have killed her. I was wondering whether another prostitute maybe worked that stroll and saw her pick somebody up and got territorial about it."

"Never. Never happen."

Actually, I agreed with Celine. But it was important that her assessment of Sandra was the same as mine. She'd known Sandra much longer. And face it, she was the one with a professional opinion on this. "Did Sandra talk about her past? She once said something to me about a boyfriend."

"She didn't have a boyfriend. Never had."

The boyfriend was completely imaginary? "She said her boyfriend hit her."

"She may have said so, but it wasn't true. It must've been her father. She was always covering up for what her father did. She never had a boyfriend until Gavin. In high school her father wouldn't let her date, and then she dropped out of school and, you know, got into this line of work. Lots of times she seemed to kind of, like, fantasize, that she had boyfriends. But I think she felt, somehow, that she wasn't entitled. Her father really had messed up her head."

"Who else would know about her family situation? She told me once there was a family doctor. She said his name was Wachstein."

"Yeah. She said something about that. Sydney Wachstein, I think."

Celine was holding her mug of coffee tightly. She was shivering a little, probably at the news about Sandra's infection.

My eyes fell on Celine's hands. They were curved around the mug of coffee. What did I know about Celine, really? Did she really like Sandra?

Maybe Sandra liked Celine, but maybe Celine had been jealous of Sandra. She had told me she frequently had to borrow money from Sandra. She had owed Sandra money at the time of her death. Sandra must have made a lot more money on the agency's "dates" than Celine. Sandra was more beautiful than Celine, so she got paid more. Celine had beautiful brown eyes with long lashes, but her chin receded more than was fashionable, given the narrow standards of beauty in our end-of-the-twentieth-century culture. She was pretty, all right, but Sandra had been beautiful.

Was that enough to cause deep, secret, violent jealousy?

I studied her hands. Her knuckles were not bruised or cut or swollen.

But then I looked down at Celine's giant handbag. If a person were to hit Sandra with a bag that heavy, then while she was stunned hit her again, no doubt she would fall backward like a log. And maybe strike her head on a curb.

A person she knew well and trusted could get close enough for that.

SEVENTEEN

THE MORE I FOUND OUT about Sandra, the more complex a person she turned out to have been. Plus smart, even though she had been very troubled. I just plain did not believe that she'd been killed by a passing stranger, or a drug dealer. No matter how young she was, she'd been streetwise too long. Regardless of how upset she might have been by the letter from the Health Department, her street smarts would not have stopped working; they would have worked automatically, on autopilot, the way most of us drive cars when we're thinking about something else.

IT WAS ONLY SEVEN OR SO blocks from Starbuck's to my place. I was worrying about Celine, about whether she could have killed Sandra, about how I could ever tell who had killed Sandra. After all, there had been a number of people more or less close that night—Gavin, Ross, Celine. Plus who could tell where Sandra's unappetizing father was? And although Gene Cirincione's office was not in this ward, it was in the next one south, and he certainly knew how to take a cab, walk, drive, or even take the anonymous El, which stopped practically within spitting distance of my place.

The hell of it was, there was no real evidence in this case. There are no ballistic markings on knuckles. Even bite marks were more distinctive than the cuts on Sandra's lip.

Damn.

But the human mind works in mysterious ways. Mine often works more slowly than I would wish. The idea came like this:

Why had I asked Celine about Sandra's doctor? What could Sandra's doctor have to contribute? What question was trying to work its way to the front of my brain?

What stairs?

Wait a minute! What stairs? Sandra said her father knocked her mother down the stairs. And they lived in a one-story bungalow!

Well, let's not get too excited here. Maybe he knocked her down the cellar stairs. There was probably a basement in that house. No, that didn't work. Sandra said her father was cheap, and that if he hadn't been so cheap and had had the stairs carpeted, her mother wouldn't have been killed. Nobody carpets cellar stairs. Or at least hardly anybody, and certainly not people in a house like the Lupicas'.

I knew better than to take anything Sandra said literally at this point. But there was something here that had to be figured out. And the only contact from that period of time, the time when Sandra's mother died, was their family doctor.

"DR. SYDNEY WACHSTEIN'S office."

I was momentarily speechless. I had expected an answering machine, this being Sunday. But here was a live human being.

"Hello. My name is Catherine Marsala. I'm a writer doing a television essay for Channel Three. I need to talk with Dr. Wachstein about a former patient—"

"Dr. Wachstein will not discuss patients with the media. No reputable physician would."

"Please. Just let me explain. This patient is dead. And the issues go beyond—"

"Ms.—Marsala, did you say? Even when the patient is deceased, it is improper to discuss their medical histories."

"Look, all I'm asking is for Dr. Wachstein to talk with me. I'll present my case. After that, we'll see. Is that too much to ask?"

Well, from her voice it seemed it was much too much to ask, but she apparently decided to treat the doctor like an adult who could make decisions, and she gave me an appointment. At six-fifteen that evening, which suggested to me she hoped Dr. Wachstein would be too tired to talk or listen to me by then anyhow.

In my line of work, we take what we can get.

THE EXTREMELY CUTE little nurse in the unfashionably tight white uniform let me into Dr. Wachstein's office. "The doctor is with a patient. It'll be a couple of minutes."

I settled down in an uneasy chair. There was no point in fretting. Dr. Wachstein was probably a dirty old man, if he asked his nurse to dress like that. On the other hand, he had the photos of two happy-looking children on his desk, a boy of maybe seven and a girl at least two years older.

A woman in a white coat came in and sat down behind the desk. I blinked.

"Uh—Dr. Wachstein?" I said, being quick on the uptake.

Unfortunately, so was she. "Expect all doctors to be male?" she said, wryly.

"Oh, come *on!* Not hardly. That's an old joke, anyhow. But why have the name Sydney?"

"Beats me. My mother was unconventional. And I know several women named Sydney. Well, two, anyway."

"While I'm at it, why are you open on Sunday?"

"This is a blue-collar neighborhood, Ms. Marsala. These people *work*. They can go to doctors evenings, Saturday, or Sunday. Personally, I take Wednesday off all day, and a half day Thursday. The morning half of Thursday."

"And why in hell do you have your nurse running around like a *Playboy* ad?"

She started to chuckle. "Muffin is a size six. I've bought her half a dozen uniforms in size eight over the last year. She says they shrink the very instant she puts them in her dryer."

Dr. Wachstein was pleasantly middle-aged, going gray, and had the calmness of a person who had either seen it all or at least a whole lot of it. I wondered whether the kids in the pictures were hers, born late after she'd finished med school and internship and so on, or the children of a son or daughter born early in her life.

"Now," she said, "do you want to explain why you're here?"

I explained. How I'd met Sandra, what she had been doing with her life, about her relationships, her short stay with me, her letter from the Board of Health, her story of her mother's fall, her toughness, her waifness, her death.

Then we stared at each other. After a good half minute, Dr. Wachstein said, "Now, do you want to explain why you're here?"

"I want to know whether he killed her. Her father. It seemed clear to me, at first, that he had. Then when I saw him the second time, it didn't seem anywhere nearly so clear. The key to the whole thing has to be Sandra's character. She was sweet. It's hard to understand how she would have enraged anybody that night. Especially that night. Except her father, who was always furious at her. It's possible whatever you might tell me would give me a pointer. Whoever did it, he shouldn't be allowed to get away with it."

"Why can't you leave it to the police?"

"I can. I will. I just want to help them a little bit, with things they don't understand as well as I do."

"Such as?"

"Damn it. Do you have to ask hard questions? I feel responsible for her, okay? Can't you just help me? How do we know that the police aren't busy with some other murder of somebody more a part of respectable society?"

"So it's 'we' now, too, is it?"

"Dr. Wachstein, you've known the Lupica family for years, I understand. Sandra's dead. Her mother's dead. How can it hurt, just to explain to me why her father was never prosecuted for shoving her mother down stairs?"

Dr. Wachstein picked up the wastebasket, put it on her desk, rummaged inside it and got out a package of cigarettes. "Don't tell me not to smoke," she said.

"I didn't say a word."

The matches were in the wastebasket, too. I stared straight at the ceiling while she lit one. Then she crumpled the pack, which still looked full, put it in the wastebasket, and put the wastebasket back on the floor.

"Telling you this is unethical," she said.

"All right."

"You will hold this in confidence."

"Yes, ma'am."

"Mr. Lupica wasn't prosecuted for pushing Mrs. Lupica down the stairs because she didn't get pushed down the stairs."

"She fell?"

"No. She died of natural causes."

"You mean no fall at all?"

"No fall at all. Although when I say natural causes, that isn't what I'd call it if I had my way. It all happened when Sandra was fourteen. Her mother developed gonorrhea."

"Her husband gave it to her."

"Right. Unfortunately, she didn't tell anybody. She must have had abdominal pain for some time. *Quite* some time. She didn't realize she was developing abdominal abscesses, but the pain must have been very severe. And eventually vomiting, chills. She was going into septicemia. By the time Sandra realized how sick her mother was and called me, the woman was in shock. We started antibiotics, of course, and went in immediately, but surgery was too late. She had massive peritonitis."

For a few seconds, I couldn't speak. Finally, I said, "I don't understand. Why didn't she tell anybody?"

"She'd caught it from her husband. She was ashamed."

"Oh. Oh, Lord."

"People don't usually die from pelvic inflammatory disease. It's serious. It can cause sterility. But it's hardly ever fatal. Her death was utterly, utterly unnecessary."

She stabbed the cigarette out, angry at herself, either for smoking or for losing a patient. Or both.

"Why didn't Sandra tell me? Why did she make up that elaborate story?"

"Pain, I suppose. It hurt her to talk about the real event. And the story about falling down the stairs probably seemed, umm, cleaner to her."

"Cleaner?"

"Yes. After all, her father'd given Sandra gonorrhea, too."

EIGHTEEN

ONE OF THE REQUIREMENTS of my job is a certain appearance of confidence. No matter whether a reporter is interviewing a subject for the print media or television, it's important that the subject feels he is in good hands, that the interviewer is a professional who has done this kind of thing many times. With more complicated, more investigative stories, I often have to extract information from reluctant people, which is something like surgery without an anesthetic, and I have to appear so knowledgeable that they believe it will be less painful to get it over with right away.

Appearing confident and actually being confident are two different things.

This entire investigation had undermined something in me, and I was feeling vulnerable. Part of it was the stress of entering a new medium, television, in a high-profile kind of way. But part of it was the subject matter. Knowing two prostitutes, however briefly, had altered the way I viewed prostitution and even sexuality. I began to realize how much difference it made that we were all starting from different places, psychologically speaking. I still believed that people were all basically alike, but the effects of different family situations were terribly important. It was too brash to decide I really knew a person's character just from acquaintance. At best, it might be possible to get an idea of personality traits. But people are still exceedingly unpredictable. Human beings are not like hard, physical data; they are not fingerprints or ballistic evidence, or chemical traces, or pollen grains. They may do one thing today and something quite different the next day. Dealing with them is probabilistic, not definite.

Each of us knows very little about what another is thinking.

And most specifically, who was I to decide on the basis of a brief conversation that Mr. Lupica had not killed his daughter? My *intuition?* How arrogant could you get?

It took me until two A.M. to fall asleep, and I woke up at four, still worrying about the same things.

Pacing around the living room didn't help; it was too small to go in any one direction for more than seven steps. Besides, LJ was trying to sleep. He eyed me several times—he can cock his head sideways, open the forward-facing eye, and look like a one-eyed monster.

At five-thirty A.M. I called Area Six. Fortunately, police departments don't sleep. It was Monday morning. The question was Would Crossley be in today, even though he'd been at work on Saturday? The answer was yes, at nine. I asked that somebody leave a note to tell him that I'd be coming in.

The deli opened at six for people who wanted breakfast before leaving for work. I got some bagels, cream cheese, and milk, and took them home. LJ will eat bread or bagels soaked in milk sometimes, even though he doesn't consider it gourmet food.

Then, with two cups of coffee in my system, I forced myself to write up notes from the last two days of interviews, including the visit to Beau Monde.

At eight-thirty I thought of calling John at work. He usually got into the office by then because the stock market in New York opens at ten, which is nine Chicago time, and he has to get his orders ready. For a while, I put it off. But waiting wasn't going to make it easier.

"Hello?"

"John, it's Cat."

"Oh." Three seconds of silence. "How are you?"

"Okay. John"—this was going to be hard—"I'm sorry. I was being rigid."

He was stunned. I don't apologize easily, and he knew it. "Well, Cat, maybe I was—no, not maybe, I was somewhat—no, not somewhat—I was rather—no, not rather—I guess I was being insensitive."

"Well." Still, apologies aside, I had to ask one thing. "John, I know you think prostitutes put themselves outside society's rules in some important way. Do you think that's equally true of their customers?"

"Of course."

"That's fair, anyhow."

"Cat, let me ask you something. How much do you think we have to agree, you and I? Do we have to agree about everything? Most things? How much?"

"I don't know."

"We can't agree on everything."

"I understand that."

Another three seconds of silence. "We'll talk."

"That's right. Let's talk about it."

We hung up. I'd tell him later what had happened to Sandra. Right now, it was just too heavy—it would add a burden to the conversation that would throw off any other discussion.

Then I drove over to Area Six.

Crossley was there, buffed up, clean-shaven, pants as sharply creased as ever, plus he'd heard that I was coming and wasn't really delighted.

"What do you want, now?"

"Hey, I didn't want anything the last time I was here. Much. I had something to give you."

"Mr. Lupica?"

"Right. I went to see him yesterday, and I thought from what he said—he sounded very normal—"

"He's out."

"What?"

"He didn't do it."

"That's what I was about to say—"

"The girl had to have been killed very shortly before she was found. Half an hour at the very top. And his next-door neighbor saw him at nine-thirty P.M."

"Really? He's not a very gregarious man."

"I said saw him. Not to talk to. The neighbor went out to turn off his hose and he saw Lupica through the living room window. He couldn't have killed her earlier and hurried home, because she wasn't killed earlier than that. And if he was there at nine-thirty, with Chicago traffic being like it is, there is *no way* he could get to North Franklin in time to kill her, even if she was killed two seconds before she was found."

"Yeah, I know. Hegewisch to the Loop can't be done that fast, even by carrier pigeon."

"However, Miss Marsala, this is not your problem."

"Oh. Are *you* getting somewhere on it?"

"That's not something I want to discuss. If you have any additional information, tell me. Otherwise, leave it to us."

"So you're not getting anywhere."

"Miss Marsala. Don't go interview Lupica. Don't try to solve this."

"I knew the victim. Some way or other, her character precipitated the murder."

"Maybe. And maybe it was random. Don't detect, Miss Marsala. You'll just get into trouble. Leave it to us."

"Thanks, Detective Crossley. I appreciate the warning."

I WASN'T SURE WHETHER to be pleased that my instinct about George Lupica was right, or unhappy that the most likely killer couldn't have done it. This forced me back to my vague worries and suspicions of the night before, a mental condition that I really shouldn't have indulged in right then.

There was work to do. I phoned Felipe.

It was now midmorning Monday. A week earlier I would not have thought there was any chance of finding hookers anywhere at this time of day. Now, Felipe and I went straight to an area just west of Wells where there was a cluster of bars. For some reason, hotel workers in the area who worked weekend nights considered these "their" bars. Since payday for them was late Sunday night, hookers hung around outside these bars Monday morning, just as hookers hang around the gates of factories on payday.

Felipe and I did a little prowling, then started to talk with hookers on the street. We wasted a lot of time getting rebuffed. We also wasted a good amount of money buying them food. For some reason, Chicago-style red hots with sauerkraut were very big around here. There was no "Eureka!" with the streetwalkers, but I did get one young woman to talk about a time when she had got into a car at night, been driven to a cemetery, and raped on a crypt. She called it rape, she said, because she hadn't been paid. "On the other hand, honey, I was so glad to see the back of that man, I din' call him back to pay me. And that's somethin', honey. I would *ordinarily* be real serious about!''

We left word at the storefront porno parlor and whorehouse that we would pay Denise sixty dollars if she'd meet us that night at the El stop near her stroll. Eleven P.M., and we'd pay only if she'd talk. The harridan who took the message said, ''Sixty bucks'll get her attention.''

We finished about five P.M., thoroughly exhausted, and rested our weary feet in a tacqueria. Then we split up to go home, to meet on the El platform at eleven.

At six I called the Eighteenth District and was utterly surprised to hear that Ross was off duty. Having run into so many people who worked Sunday, it seemed like a personal affront that he didn't work on Monday, a perfectly normal workday. But since he worked weekends, it was only fair. Fortunately, I had his beeper number. I dialed it.

When he phoned me back, I said, ''Any possibility of you meeting me and Felipe tonight about eleven?''

''Hey! I'm off today.''

''We located the hooker. And we might need your help.''

''I got television I want to watch.''

''I'll buy late dinner. Steak house on Michigan.''

''Oh. Well, maybe that's different.''

''Okay.'' Maybe he was getting addicted to free meals on Channel Three. ''Don't bring Gavin, though. I'd like to talk with you about him.''

''Hey, he ain't grafted to my backside, you know.''

''Thanks, Ross.''

''You pay, I play.''

He was such a flatterer.

NINETEEN

THE EL STATION was a perfect setting for an interview with a streetwalker, especially since we had already used an actual street for the setting of one of the other women. The El in this part of town runs very high up— it's *really* elevated. It's at the third-floor level of the apartments around here. If you're riding along, you feel almost indecent seeing into everybody's bedrooms.

This area of Franklin Street is largely art galleries. Some have closed because of the recession. Others were just closed now because it was late at night. I was standing on the platform, and the tracks, high in the air, stretched off in both directions. About a block away was the curve that El makes at Chicago Avenue. So in that direction, the receding tracks looked like a foreshortened S.

The blocks of darkened buildings obscured some of the skyline. Not all. I could see Chicago Avenue stretching away toward the high-rent district, the ninety-six-story John Hancock and Water Tower Place looming above in the distance. The peach-colored streetlights beneath the station made patterns on the sides of the crosspieces of the tracks. These are wooden railroad ties strung across metal girders, so there is space between each tie and the next, and the streetlights below shone up through the gaps.

The El platform was also lighted, gloomily, with widely separated bluish bar lights on high stanchions.

These created pools of light on the platform, with dimmer spaces between.

Given the blue pools from the platform lights and the peculiar pinkish beams that shone up between the tracks, this would be the most atmospheric shot of all in the television essay, if Felipe could get his camera to capture it. He thought he could. A hooker half-lit in this environment would illustrate the phrase ''lady of the night'' to perfection.

During the day, when El tickets were sold in the ground-floor station, you had to have a ticket to go through the turnstile and come up the stairs. At this time of night, you paid on the train. Which was fine with us, because Ross had warned us that no prostitute was going to pay for a ticket to get up here to talk with us. Now she could just walk up. Also, it reflected the fact that, even though this was a very busy station at rush hour, hardly anybody used it this time of night. We'd be alone up here, most of the time.

Felipe and I had picked it for that reason, and because it was one of the few stations that still had one or two benches. Most benches in most El stations had been removed so that street people would not sleep on them. We figured we'd want to sit down for the interview.

Right now there was one lone man standing near the edge of the platform, huddled in a leather jacket, despite the fact that it wasn't really cold. I hoped he wasn't despondent. I didn't want to try to stop somebody from jumping in front of a train.

Every once in a while a sigh of damp breeze came along the tracks, bringing with it a smell of oil and metal.

There was a sound of footsteps on the metal stairs. Solid and determined footsteps. I knew it was Felipe before I saw his dark hair rise up in the stairwell, followed by shoulders laden with camera straps.

"Hiya," I said.

"Got everything," Felipe said. "Our subject here yet?"

"Nope. Beautiful atmosphere, though."

"Well, let's see."

His reaction to the strange and brooding lighting effects was a lot more cautious than mine, probably because he had to actually photograph them. "Nice contrast," he finally conceded. "The figure, silhouetted against the tracks. That bluish light coming down and then the reddish beams spreading up between the tracks like—"

"—the fires of hell?" I suggested, enthusiastically.

"I would have said volcanic action," Felipe said. "But definitely evocative, you betcha."

"And the audio—"

"Well, it depends how close we stand to all this metal platform backing, but I bet we get a pretty good sound."

A northbound train roared in, and the man in the leather jacket got onto it without throwing himself under the wheels. A great relief. The train started up immediately and left the station. Two women in long raincoats carrying stuffed paper bags, lumpy with unknown contents, trudged up the steps to the southbound station on the other side. The sounds made by their feet were quite different from Felipe's—no wonder I had recognized his. Their feet sounded tired.

"Yo!" It was Ross. His footsteps had been covered by the women's.

"Hi, Ross," I said.

"What's new? You got our girl?"

"Not yet."

He looked around the El station. This was his patch, after all. He sat down on the bench. A southbound train was coming in, metal wheels shrieking on the metal track, brakes starting to catch, making the whole platform vibrate. It screamed to a stop, like fingernails making a last scrape at a blackboard. The two women got on. They didn't speak to each other, but moved together and clearly knew each other.

"Well, tape's ready," Felipe said, unnecessarily. Felipe always had tape ready.

"When's she supposed to get here?" Ross asked.

"By eleven."

"Eleven now," he said.

"Actually, *before* eleven is what she said."

"Oh, just swell. Now we're waiting on the word of one of the least reliable people on earth," Ross grumbled.

"Well, we won't wait forever. We'll go eat. Anyhow, hookers must be able to get places on time for appointments with tricks," I said.

"You're thinking of call girls. These here street hostesses can't walk and pop their bra strap at the same time."

Felipe settled back on the bench and said, "Oh, excellent!" We waited.

A northbound train came screaming in, hissed at the station, and grumbled out again, without picking anybody up. We waited some more.

"This could go on forever," Ross said.

"Hey, I'm gonna feed you. This isn't such bad duty."

"I could be—"

"I know. Watching television. Gimme a break. You don't have anything else to do, either."

"Either?"

"Well," I said, "neither do I."

"I do," Felipe said. It was now eleven-fifteen.

"What?" I asked.

"I have a date."

"What time?"

"Well, I said I'd be home at quarter of twelve. But it's half an hour from here."

"Big date?" I asked.

"You betcha."

I said, "Ten minutes more?"

"Okay."

We waited while two more trains pulled through. One was an express that roared past without stopping. The only thing coming up the stairs now was a cold breeze. "Maybe we'll just have to use the bleepable lady," I said.

Ross asked, "What's the bleepable lady?" Felipe explained about our interview with the woman whose every third word was an Anglo-Saxon expletive. And how cutting it to usable material made it worse than Swiss cheese.

I looked at my watch again. "Jeez! Eleven-forty-five! Go ahead, Felipe," I said. "We did our best."

He was about to fold up his reflectors when we heard steps—little, determined steps that sounded angry, short chops at the stairs. A blond head tipped with silver glitter came into view. This had to be our hooker. I almost said, "You're late," but then I saw her face—swollen and covered with blood on the right side.

"Denise?" I said.

"Damn right. I look really great, don't I?" She laughed harshly.

"Sit down. What happened to you?"

Felipe, with his eye more on the ball than mine was, said, "Will you talk for the camera?"

"Goddamn right I will!" She sat on the bench where the lights were set up, and I realized that she was furious. I had left word that I would pay her, which was the only reason she showed up at all, but even the three twenty-dollar bills I handed her didn't tamp down her anger. She signed the studio release with a vicious scrawl. Felipe had the lights on in seconds, realizing she was volatile. Her feet in the little silver boots stamped up and down on the cement.

"What happened to you?" I asked again.

"I get in this guy's car. A guy in an expensive goddamn three-piece suit, too. And a tie! He drives around into an alley. I'm supposed to—" This part we were going to bleep out, but it was dreadfully vivid. "So I get going and he reaches down and starts strangling me. I mean his fucking thumbs were digging into my neck here—" She cocked her head up and showed deep red marks on her throat just under her chin.

"Go on."

"So I start thrashing around. No room in that goddamn Toyota anyhow! He's screaming 'Hold still and die!' Can you believe it! I cut my head on his gearshift, broke the shitty thing, hit him in the nose with my head, shit!" She was starting to cry, she was so mad. She jumped up.

"Can we use this—"

"Yeah, you just go right ahead and use this! You do that! You tell 'em. You tell 'em how it is, this life!"

"Do you want me to get you a taxi?"

"Hey! I ain't goin' home! I gotta wash up. Fucking guy didn't pay. I'm money short!"

She stomped on down the stairs, trailing the F-word after her, repeated over and over. It sounded like shots from a silenced automatic.

Felipe sighed with satisfaction and folded his reflectors, packed his bag, and put the lens cap on his videocam. The whole process took him thirty seconds.

"'Night, Felipe," I called after him as he went down the stairs.

Ross got to his feet and said, "Dinnertime!"

"One-track mind. Let me ask you something for a minute. Out of Felipe's hearing."

"What's Felipe got to do with anything?"

"I just don't want this to get back to Gavin. Ross, you know Gavin was pretty attracted to Sandra."

"Attracted? He was bug-eyed. About a *hooker!*"

"Yes. Well, that was the way it was. She had told him she was giving up the life. Anyway, what I want to know is this. Suppose he came along the street that night and he saw Sandra in the alley with a man."

"Yeah? So?"

"Suppose she was just buying some coke, but from the way they were standing or the angle or whatever, he thought they were—um—"

"Turning a trick?"

"Maybe. Would he have been enraged?"

"You think he killed her?"

"Not necessarily. I'm just *asking*. I want to know what you think."

"Hell." Another train pulled in, opened its doors, and a grubby teenager got out, crossed the platform, and was gone before the doors closed. The train accelerated and vanished.

"Because if he hit her," I said, "there's another problem."

"What?"

"Whoever hit her split her lip so hard he must have cut his hand on her teeth. And got her blood in the cut.

She'd just had a letter from the Health Department, Ross. She had the AIDS virus.''

''Oh, shit!'' Ross yelled, pulling back his sleeve and staring at his knuckle.

TWENTY

I LEAPED BACK, but Ross was quick, quicker than I thought he could be, with his overweight and bulk. He jumped between me and the stairs.

I countered his move by backing sideways, away from him, fast. But this took me farther away from the stairs, toward the dead end of the waiting platform. He bulled toward me, head lowered, fist drawn back, and I had no doubt that he wanted to hit me, then throw me off the platform, twenty-five feet to the concrete pavement below. He'd figure that there was just a chance he could pass that off as an accident.

Which meant he wouldn't get out his gun unless he had to.

I yelled, "Help!" Then I remembered something I'd read. Citizens who wouldn't get involved in a mugging would still respond to something else. I yelled, "Fire! Fire!"

But there would be few people to hear. Besides, this took only a second or two, and by now I was all the way to the back of the platform and he was coming toward me like a mountain. There was nowhere to go but the track. I jumped.

I wasn't sure which was the live rail. I thought I remembered that it was partly covered, to avoid electrocution of people who fell, but I didn't know if that was true down the whole line and I didn't have time to look. I jumped onto the space between the rails, and ran about ten feet along the track.

The railroad ties were about eight inches wide and spaced about ten inches apart. Irregularly spaced. The gap varied enough so I had to watch my footing. I was jumping onto every other one, trying desperately not to fall into the gap between. When I had gone about twenty feet I turned around, hoping to see that Ross had given up.

He was out in the middle of the tracks, drawing his gun.

I turned to face him. Though the ties weren't evenly spaced, I tried backing quickly from one to the next, keeping my eye on Ross all the time. It had only been a few seconds, even now, since this whole nightmare began, and it was far too soon for help to arrive.

There's a study done for police officers I once read about that tells how far a bad guy can run in the time it takes an officer to pull a gun from a holster. It's something like thirty feet. But they hadn't done it backing along railroad ties high over a street. I turned and sprinted, leaping two ties at once, feet hitting every third. The light from the station didn't reach this far, and I was in partial dark. Good—make it harder for Ross to see. But the orange light from the streetlights below flashed up between the ties, and as I ran, it flickered into my eyes, then off as a tie intervened, then another flash. It was a strobe effect and was making me dizzy. It was hard to tell cross tie from shadow. The breeze blew my hair in my eyes, making visibility worse.

My foot slipped.

I missed the next tie and went down, falling painfully onto the left shoulder. My right foot caught between two ties and twisted sideways.

That instant, I heard the shot. I struggled up and realized my shoulder had been hit by a round from Ross's

gun, hit before I heard the sound. Maybe falling had
saved me. Or maybe if I hadn't fallen I wouldn't have
been hit. I risked a glance as I struggled fast to my feet.
I was still in big trouble. Ross was striding after me,
cautious on the ties, confident that he had the gun and
would soon have a good clear shot. He could take his
time.

Back on the platform, Felipe burst into sight, clearly
visible in the spill of light from the platform.

"Halt!" he called. He must've seen too many movies. Ross didn't halt.

Felipe had his videocam pointed at Ross. But he
hauled off and lobbed one of his folded lights at Ross.
The thing sailed up into the air. Ross saw it coming and
sprinted a couple of steps closer to me. The light fell just
where he had been standing before. Then Ross slipped
and fell to his knees.

Felipe jumped from the platform onto the ties. But we
were half a block away from him now, Ross had a gun,
and Felipe would never catch up in time.

Ross got to his feet. He whipped around and fired off
a shot at Felipe. Felipe lurched to his left but stayed on
his feet. I hoped to hell he wasn't hit.

Ross turned back to me, and now he walked fast but
methodically, leveling his gun straight at me. A shot
chunked into a wooden tie. I turned and ran, trying to
weave, approaching the Chicago Avenue curve. Every
second or so I glanced over my shoulder. Felipe tripped
and fell. And screamed. He was hurt.

There was nothing I could do about that. I ducked and
bobbed, rounding the curve, trying not to fall through
the openings between the ties. Once my foot went
through, between the ties, and as I caught my weight on

the other foot, I looked down to the pavement far below. A car slipped past in the night. I staggered up again.

It was like jumping from rung to rung of a horizontal ladder. Except that besides trying to step on the rungs, I was also trying not to step on the rails. One of them was electrified and I didn't know which. Maybe I should just jump off—anything was better than being shot or fried. I was looking for a place I could jump from the track without falling all the way to the street—either to a neighboring building's fire escape or even onto the stanchion of a streetlight. But they were all at least ten feet away. Another shot spanged off one of the tracks.

And ahead there was the light of an oncoming train.

Oh, my God!

It was just turning into the distant south end of the Chicago Avenue curve, metal shrieking on metal. The light in the front of the train swept the buildings on the outside of the curve, then swung back and out over the emptiness of Chicago Avenue, then swung to the buildings again. I looked desperately at the other, southbound track, but it was too far to jump to. I glanced behind me for an escape route—could I possibly outrace it? But there was Ross. He had seen the train, too, and was briefly frozen, his face a caricature of startled terror.

Should I leap off the track and take my chances falling to the street below? No! It was just too far. And there was no time to run.

I dropped to the ties, thinking of wedging myself down between them. Maybe I could hang by my hands from the bottom of the ties while the train roared overhead, then pull myself back up after it passed.

Flat on my stomach between the tracks, I knew there was no time for that either. If I hunched over to wriggle into the ten-inch space between the ties, the rushing train would decapitate me.

I lay flat. Flat as possible, trying not to tremble, or twitch, or jump with shock. I buried my face between two of the ties, wedged my toes under the tie at the bottoms of my feet, stretched my arms over my head and curled my fingers down over the farthermost tie I could reach. And hung on. Would the train be high enough to clear my body, or would it pick me up, roll me, and cut me to ribbons?

The El train came on me that instant, like a tornado. The ties I lay on shimmied. The shrieking of metal and hiss of the speed combined with a whump of displaced air, as if all the air at the front of the train was compacted and bore down with a physical weight. The pressure hit my ears, not so much sound as pain. Things pinged at me from the wheels, sparks flew from the metal wheels hitting the track, and a metal piece, maybe a trailing bit of chain or wire, struck my elbow. It almost made me leap up, but I knew that way was death, and I clutched harder at the ties with my fingers and toes, willing myself to stay flat, not to move, not to give in to the panic and a terrible, almost irresistible desire to get it over with. Just jump up and be dead, and no longer saturated with fear.

It passed. I was still alive. I tilted my head, still too fearful to lift it up. Farther down the track, I could see under the train—because all this was taking hours in my mind—a view of Ross lying on the track. Lying flat as I had been. But he was much larger, much fatter than I.

I saw the image of his head go confusing, jumbled, a mix of red and clothing colors, and sparks from the wheels, and screaming brakes. I saw the train pass over him, and even as it did, things came rolling out from under the wheels, kicked out by the rolling and tossing—a shoe, a piece of something with a rag of blue cloth attached, a piece of something that looked like a cut of beef, liquid things, soft things.

Under the metal roar and scream of the train itself were chopping sounds, slapping, wet sounds.

I stood up at last.

What had happened to Felipe?

I was shaking so hard, I could scarcely stand. It was nearly impossible to walk on the ties, to hit each tie accurately with a foot.

The only way back to safety was past Ross—over Ross—through what was left of Ross. But I had to get off those tracks. I told myself no other train would come down the track, but I didn't believe it. Already the engineer was out of the cab, and there were flashlight beams darting around. The train that had hit Ross would stay where it was; there would have to be an investigation; all other trains would be routed around it.

I told myself that and it was still no use. I had to get off the track, *now!*

Over the parts of what was left of Ross, I stepped without looking. The train turned out to be three cars, plenty of room behind it for me to climb back on the platform.

And there was Felipe.

"I *tried!*" he said. The whole front of his head was covered in blood. His shirt front was a red bib.

"What happened to you?"

"I fell. I think I broke my nose."

"Yes, I think you did." It leaned off center and was swelling and dark red.

"I *tried* to stop him."

"I know you did. I saw you." Amazingly, the video-cam was still in his hand. "I see you never let go of that."

"Yeah. Forgot I had it for a while."

"Get anything?"

He grinned, not even wincing at what the grin must have cost his nose.

"You betcha! I wouldn't be surprised if I got the whole goddamn business."

TWENTY-ONE

HE WAS RIGHT. He had taped the whole damned business. Including the part where Ross fired at Felipe. It was not a smooth video, of course. This was cinema even more verité than the whorehouse. But it certainly answered every question anybody had later about what had happened to Ross.

And indirectly, about what had happened to Sandra.

The tape itself was the hottest thing on the news Tuesday morning. Felipe was the news photographer of the hour, with offers from New York pouring in. He handled it all with great dignity, modesty, and a modest, dignified request to Zucrow for a raise.

I didn't do too badly out of the tape, either. We knew for sure the upcoming prostitution segment would have a huge viewership. This took the pressure from Zucrow off my back, at the same time leaving me with the knowledge that if I messed up lots of people would be watching.

"SO BASICALLY, you had arranged this little trap with Felipe," McCoo growled Tuesday morning. He was not pleased.

"Well, of course!"

"And you decoyed Ross up onto the El, did your interview, and then got Ross by himself intentionally."

"Well, either Denise would show up or she wouldn't. After that, Felipe and I planned to wait until there weren't any other passengers, and then he'd pretend to leave and go down about four stairs and aim his camera through the railing at us and start videotaping me hitting Ross with the news that Sandra had the virus—"

"So you planned to be basically alone with Ross. Who you figured was a killer."

"Well, I didn't think he'd attack me if other people were standing around watching! And if he didn't make *some* move, he could go on stonewalling forever on Sandra's murder. He'd say he didn't do it, and there was really nothing to prove he did."

"I'll repeat myself. You *led* him to attack you?"

"Right."

"Now, that was supremely stupid, wasn't it?"

"Well, no, like I said, Felipe was waiting down the stairs. With his videocam aimed at us."

"And too far away to be *any help at all in time!*"

"Uh—but, McCoo—see, Ross was fat and clumsy. There wasn't any way he could actually catch me. I'm not all that athletic, but I knew he was dangerous and I was on the alert."

"He didn't have to catch you. He could shoot you."

"It was dark. I could run down the stairs."

"Except that you couldn't. He headed you off."

"Well, there was that one little glitch."

"*Glitch?* You were idiotically reckless!"

"It worked, didn't it? I was right."

"Wrong! Dumb! Stupid! *Utterly moronic!*"

I went over and put an arm around his shoulders and kissed his cheek. "That's okay, McCoo. Yell. Let it out. I'd be pretty upset if you got killed, too."

"*Aarrgh!*"

"Now you sound like LJ."

He lurched back into his chair. He was puffing his lips in and out, like Nero Wolfe was said to do. I assumed this was a temper-containing device. Time passed. His breathing slowed. After a couple of minutes, he said, "This is Kenyan mocha java."

He was making peace. Good. I picked up the pot of mocha java and poured us each a cup. He said more mildly, "If that shot had been six inches farther right, you'd be dead instead of just barely nicked."

"Six inches?" I said. The slight graze, thank heavens, had required four stitches, but no major repairs. "That's plenty. You know, McCoo, every time you're driving down a street, there you are, passing cars coming the other way, with maybe a couple of feet between you. Your combined speeds may be a hundred or more. A head-on would be certain death."

"So?"

"So you can't spend much time in this life thinking about close calls."

"Mmmm. You're waxing philosophical now, huh?"

"Might as well."

McCoo said, "Did you suspect Ross when I told you about his brutality complaints?"

"No. Not at all. They weren't against women, and so they weren't really related. I thought it was Gavin."

"Gavin Lowenthal? Why? He didn't have any history of excessive force."

"I thought he'd fallen hard for Sandra, and he believed she'd given up prostitution, and then he'd come on her that night and either saw her with somebody or misinterpreted whatever he saw. And killed her in a rage. It took a couple of things to make me realize she wouldn't have been 'close' to anybody."

"The HIV test?"

"Well, yes, once I knew about that. The point was, put the AIDS test together with what her father had done to her mother and Sandra, infecting them both—it seemed to me the conclusion was pretty final. You

never really *know* anything about people. As LJ sometimes says, 'There's nowt so strange as folk.' It's not like
you can work people out on a chessboard.''

''You can say that again.''

''But everything I knew about Sandra told me that she
was not heartless, not cruel, not hurtful to anybody who
hadn't been hurtful to her. The only person she really
hated, and half loved, was her father. Once she found
out that she had the AIDS virus, I did *not* believe she
would have had sex with anybody. So Gavin would not
have seen her having sex in the alley. And since she
bought the coke at the deli, there had to be another reason she was in the alley.''

''Cirincione? Why couldn't she have been meeting
him? We have a woman who's willing to give evidence
against him, by the way.''

''Good.''

''I suspect he got into the 'Sinless Seven' either as a
good cover or because he'd just as soon see the street
hookers out of business, leaving the arena to his own
women.''

''Serves him right if you charge him. But I didn't think
he would be in an alley with Sandra. See, the other thing
Sandra was, was smart. I doubted that she would call
Cirincione and then believe him if he said he could get a
whole lot of money in an hour or two. And even if he
said he was bringing her a small down payment, she
certainly wouldn't have gone into an alley alone with
him.''

''She was street smart. I agree. Had to be to survive.''

''So who else was around? Celine? I thought about it,
but she didn't show any signs of resenting Sandra, and
besides, I think Sandra would have told her about the
AIDS virus the minute she saw her. After which, Celine
would hardly envy her any longer.''

"Hardly. The poor woman. Sandra couldn't have died happy."

"No." I sipped coffee. There was nothing to be done for Sandra anymore. "I realized—late, I admit—that what Gavin had been saying about Ross all along was right. He was as nasty as he seemed. I had thought it was a kind of dumb male-chauvinist act."

"Naive of you."

"That's what Gavin said. I knew Ross sometimes had sex with prostitutes, probably in exchange for not running them in. And I knew he divided women into two categories, whores and good girls. And since Sandra was a whore, she could be forced to have sex. As he put it about one of the other hookers, she didn't lose anything she valued, did she? And if she refused, since she didn't have any *principled* reason for turning him down, she was just slapping him in the face."

"Which infuriated him."

"Right. He asked her into the alley to talk. Then he demanded sex in the alley. When she refused, he thought she was just spitting at him personally. When, really, it was a combination of what she had promised Gavin, first, and then second, the fact that she knew she had the virus."

"She was protecting Ross?"

"I wouldn't be a bit surprised. And although she could have told him, when he started to force her, she probably got so angry that she just pushed him away. And he hit her. Two or three times."

"Cat, it's possible that Ross wanted sex with her partly to show Gavin, to be one up on his partner. I told you he had problems with partners. He was competitive with them. To the point of fighting."

"Or to show the kid in the nastiest way possible what the world was really like."

McCoo thought a few seconds. "Yeah. But I'd bet on my interpretation."

"I had thought Ross was the male chauvinist with the heart of gold. But he wasn't. All he needed to do, and this never would have happened, is realize Sandra was a human being."

"Where was he gonna learn?"

"What do you mean?"

"I knew his father. He was a sergeant in the Eighteenth when I was starting out. An old-style police officer. Hit 'em and pull 'em in. This is the type who hits his wife and keeps his kids in line with more of the same."

"You're saying—"

"Ross probably had a hellish childhood. Where was he gonna learn gentleness?"

"He *should* have learned it. Later on. Other people do."

"There are a lot of people out there who are raised in a certain way and after that never really learn anything else, ever, any other way of behaving."

"They ought to. Otherwise, you're saying it's all just hopeless. Everything is preordained. All these tragedies, one after the other, will just go on happening forever, passed on from parent to child."

"That's what's been happening, hasn't it? Since time began?"

"Now who's waxing philosophical?" I smiled, but lost the smile right away. "I don't like that. I don't like to think that way."

"It doesn't really matter whether you like it or not, does it, Cat?"

ON TUESDAY AFTERNOON we edited some more clips and taped my closing remarks. It's astonishing how being close to death diminishes in your mind the importance of just how your hair looks on a TV program. I felt far more in control taping the ending than I had been three days earlier. I hoped the viewer wouldn't think I'd mellowed miraculously between the first minute of the piece and the eighth minute.

They were now giving me ten minutes, a very big deal in television, because of the media play resulting from Ross's death, the popularity of Felipe's tape, and on top of all that the sudden news of Gene Cirincione's arrest.

I said to the camera: "All of the women I interviewed either believed or said they believed that they were engaging in prostitution only long enough to accumulate enough money to go into a legitimate business. All the women I interviewed were from family situations that did not provide them with a nest egg or a start in a business or profession. And all the women I interviewed had accumulated next to no money, no matter how long they had been prostitutes. And all gave from fifty to ninety percent of the money they earned to their pimp, service, or boyfriend. The rest went into clothes and drugs or alcohol, which they used constantly. The drugs and alcohol were both cause and effect. They could have been the reason the women could not hold regular jobs in the first place, but in most cases the chemical help seemed to have come later, as a way of getting through the nastiness of their work."

WHEN THE SEGMENT AIRED, it didn't show any of the difficulty that had gone into making it. And it didn't show any seams, either. It looked smooth. Amazing!

The *Trib* said in its review, which always precedes the public showing by a day, "What makes this television essay so compelling, and at the same time so horrifying, is the fact that it is so businesslike. Prostitution is a business, not a game, and not, to its workers, recreation. Marsala has painted it as it is. A dangerous business."

The *Sun-Times* said, "It wouldn't be a bad thing for this short documentary to be shown in high schools. We don't like to think about it, but a number of the young girls you see in the eighth, ninth, and tenth grades may already be making money as prostitutes or will soon start. It's just possible that this television essay might deter a few girls from entering the life. They need to know that prostitution, even at the high end, is not glamorous, that you can't go into it thinking that you will make some money and open a legitimate business later, because you won't. You won't make money. And there may not be a later."

THAT NEXT SATURDAY I was playing attack-the-Nerf-ball with LJ when Celine came calling. "Hey! I've been thinking about you," I said.

"Yeah. I've been thinking about you."

"Naturally. You must have been, since you're here." We both laughed.

"I've been thinking about maybe getting out of—you know, getting another kind of job."

"I sure as hell wish you would."

"I mean, that AIDS business! I kind of like adventure, but that's not adventure. That's more like suicide. I kind of learned something about myself, thinking about Sandra."

"Want to know what I was thinking about you?"

"Yeah."

"Have you ever been arrested for a felony?"

She was puzzled. "No. Misdemeanor. Not a *felony*. Why?"

"I did an article on firefighters last year. About women firefighters in Chicago. It's got some high-risk moments. But they don't take applications from anybody who's been convicted of a felony."

"Firemen, huh?" Celine said.

"Firefighters."

She smiled and said, "Hey. Heeeeeeey."

I'D LEARNED SOMETHING about myself, too. My whole misunderstanding of Ross's character was based on some kind of optimism or innocence that I didn't think I possessed. To me, I seemed worldly wise, experienced, and professional. But I had been completely unable to believe that he was as deeply bigoted as he said he was. When he made crude remarks, I believed he was joking, even when there was no indication that he really *was* joking. Was I dumb enough to think the whole world was composed of good guys?

FINALLY, on Sunday, Hermione came over, bringing her new puppy to show me.

Long John hates pets, all pets, not just cats. He hates dogs, too, and he probably would hate horses if he saw one. Long John considers pets to be things that have four feet. He doesn't consider himself a pet anyway, of course, and besides that, he's got two feet.

Hermione and her Dalmatian came bounding up the stairs and into the apartment. The puppy was a darling, about four months old. Pink tongue lolling, white silky coat, black spots. Hermione said, "Dalmatians are born white, and they develop the spots as they grow. He's had his markings for several weeks now. Isn't he a *beauty?*"

Long John Silver threw the creature a horrified glance from one of his wise, wrinkled eyes, flew up onto the curtain rod, and screamed, "Out, out damned spot!"

SOMEBODY'S DEAD IN SNELLVILLE

PATRICIA HOUCK SPRINKLE

A Sheila Travis Mystery

First Time in Paperback

OVER HER DEAD BODY

The small Georgia town does little more than straggle along the Atlanta-Athens highway in an endless chain of national franchises. But big opportunities are knocking. The faded glory of the Sims family is about to be restored when major developers offer Grandma Sims ten million dollars for the family homestead. However, the ninety-seven-year-old matriarch won't sell.

But that doesn't stop murder from striking down members of the immediate family, and involving Sheila in a web of killings that gives new meaning to the phrase *family plot.*

"Sprinkle has...a good eye for depicting rural Southern life...." —*Publishers Weekly*

Available in August at your favorite retail stores.

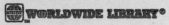

THE DOWN HOME *Heifer Heist*

Eve K. SANDSTROM

First Time in Paperback

A Sam & Nicky Titus Mystery

THIN ICE

Rancher Joe Pilkington, neighbor to Sheriff Sam Titus and photographer wife Nicky, is run down when he interrupts rustlers during a heist. Aside from tire tracks in the snow, the only clue is the sound of Mozart heard playing from the killer's truck.

Two more grisly deaths follow, and it looks as if a beloved member of the Titus ranch may be accused of murder. Sam and Nicky grimly set out to corner a killer...before they become victims themselves.

"Sandstrom makes the most of her setting...."
—Publishers Weekly

Available in October at your favorite retail stores.

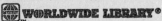

CAT'S CRADLE
CLARE CURZON

A Mike Yeadings Mystery

OLD LORELY PELLING WAS AS QUEER AS TWO LEFT BOOTS....

She's a reclusive eccentric with a checkered past and dozens of cats, and her shooting death is first believed accidental, the result of local boys' target practice. But Detective Superintendent Mike Yeadings of the Thames Valley Police Force believes darker motives are behind the death of the old woman.

The villagers are astounded that Lorely has named her neighbor's children sole inheritors of her estate. For Yeadings, it means unraveling the tangled skein of deception, scandal and desperation in Lorely's long, frustrated life—and the secrets she shared with a killer.

"All the right ingredients." —*Booklist*

Available in September at your favorite retail stores.

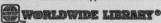